Out of sight, out of mind . . .

Nina watched as Ryan Taylor pulled on a Sweet Valley Shore T-shirt over his tanned, muscled chest. He looked over the faces gathered around him. When he saw Nina, Ryan smiled briefly and winked his recognition. "I'm Ryan Taylor, and I'm the head of the Sweet Valley Shore Squad," he announced to the crowd of potential lifeguards who'd gathered around him.

Nina grinned. Ryan was an intense guy. Complex. Hard to predict. A total hunk who could make your life a living hell. Or he could completely make your day.

Nina cut her eyes toward Elizabeth, hoping to exchange a look of triumph at how well things were working out. They'd moved into an amazing beach house. They had enough people to cover the costs, and were about to have a great summer with a group of their favorite people from SVU. But Elizabeth was too busy to catch her best friend's stare. Nina saw Elizabeth's glassy gaze glued to Ryan's perfectly chiseled face. *Wow!* Elizabeth seemed to have it bad for the elusive head lifeguard. *Has Elizabeth forgotten about boyfriend Tom before the summer has even officially begun?*

Bantam Books in the Sweet Valley University series
Ask your bookseller for the books you have missed

And don't miss these Sweet Valley
University Thriller Editions:

SWEET VALLEY UNIVERSITY®

For the Love of Ryan

Written by
Laurie John

Created by
FRANCINE PASCAL

BANTAM BOOKS
NEW YORK · TORONTO · LONDON · SYDNEY · AUCKLAND

To Kimberly Bloom

RL 6, age 12 and up

FOR THE LOVE OF RYAN
A Bantam Book / June 1996

Sweet Valley High® *and Sweet Valley University*®
are registered trademarks of Francine Pascal
Conceived by Francine Pascal
Produced by Daniel Weiss Associates, Inc.
33 West 17th Street
New York, NY 10011

ISBN: 0-553-56704-7

Published simultaneously in the United States and Canada

Bantam Books are published by Bantam Books, a division of Bantam
Doubleday Dell Publishing Group, Inc. Its trademark, consisting of the
words "Bantam Books" and the portrayal of a rooster, is Registered in
U.S. Patent and Trademark Office and in other countries. Marca
Registrada. Bantam Books, 1540 Broadway, New York, New York 10036.

PRINTED IN THE UNITED STATES OF AMERICA

OPM   0 9 8 7 6 5 4 3 2 1

Chapter One

"Ooo, baby! Those guys hanging out by the Sweet Valley Shore sign were hot," Jessica Wakefield said as she stepped out of the red Jeep. "Did you see them waving at us as we drove by?"

"Maybe you didn't notice," her twin sister, Elizabeth, began, "but I was busy driving. My eyes were on the road, not on the hunks." Elizabeth rolled her head around on her neck, glad their long trip was over. Her muscles felt bunched and tense after several hours behind the steering wheel.

Elizabeth hoisted her duffel bag and started up the stairs of the three-story Victorian beach house, eager to find a room and get settled in.

"Well, you really missed a great view," Jessica commented happily. "I wonder who they were. I hope I'll be seeing lots more of them."

"If they're here for the same reason we're here, I'm sure you'll be seeing them around."

"You mean they're here for sun, fun, romance, and nonstop partying, too?"

"No, silly . . . work," Elizabeth corrected. "Some of us actually plan to make some money lifeguarding this summer." She reached the top of the stairs and paused on the landing, where a large window was half open. Elizabeth took a deep breath, enjoying the salty ocean scent.

"Oh, yeah, lifeguarding. Hey, I've got dibs on the room with the view," Jessica shouted from the bottom of the stairs. "Especially if it has a view of those gorgeous beach bums."

Elizabeth looked out the window on the landing. Several cars were parked outside the house next door. But she didn't see anybody around. "Wow!" she said in a loud voice. "Look at the abs on *that* guy."

"What guy?"

Elizabeth heard Jessica's feet clatter quickly up the stairs.

"Over there." Elizabeth pointed out the window. "Don't you see him? He's got long, wavy brown hair. Shoulders like Hercules. And—"

The next thing she knew Jessica was standing at her elbow, peering over her shoulder. "Where? Where?"

Elizabeth laughed. "Gotcha."

Jessica pressed her lips together. "Ha, ha!" she said sarcastically. "Very funny. But I'll bet there are tons of major hunks at Sweet Valley Shore. And if

2

I don't meet one before the day is over, my name's not Jessica Wakefield."

"What's in here?" Elizabeth asked as she pushed open the door on the right of the landing.

"A mess!" Jessica exclaimed, following close on Elizabeth's heels.

Elizabeth's eyebrows shot up in surprise as she recognized Nina Harper's toiletries and books flung on the bureau and the floor. Her large suitcase lay open beside the unmade bed, only half unpacked.

Nina, Elizabeth's best friend, had arrived yesterday to take possession of the house from the owner, Mrs. Krebbs. Elizabeth knew Nina was a semicertified neat freak. The disarray probably meant she'd been beyond busy since she had arrived. Too busy to unpack her clothes and tidy the attractive, old-fashioned room.

Elizabeth's glance took in the yellow walls, high white ceiling, and polished dark wood floors. The window was open, and white muslin curtains billowed gracefully like sails in the breeze.

"Great room," Elizabeth said.

"I'm going downstairs to get my suitcase," Jessica said, clattering back down the stairs.

Elizabeth walked across the landing. The door on the other side of the landing was opened a crack, so she peeked inside and stepped in. The rose-patterned wallpaper coordinated with the hooked rugs in red, pink, white, and yellow that were

3

scattered on the floor. The headboard on the bed was iron with an intricate design. Sheets, a colorful red-and-yellow quilt, and a thick feather pillow were piled neatly at the foot of the bare mattress.

The windows of one wall faced the ocean. And the windows of the other wall faced the dunes.

Since the room was clearly unoccupied and available, Elizabeth quickly dropped her duffel bag on the floor, walked over to the old-fashioned dressing table, and examined her reflection in the mirror.

Her shoulder-length blond ponytail was pulled through the back of a billed Sweet Valley University baseball cap. The cap's bill had done a pretty good job of protecting her nose during the long drive with the Jeep's top down. But her delicately chiseled tip was definitely pinker than it had been earlier that morning.

They'd driven down in the open red Jeep that Elizabeth and her identical twin, Jessica, shared. Winston Egbert, a friend and fellow housemate for the summer, had ridden with them—napping in the backseat for most of the trip.

Elizabeth felt as if she could use a nap herself, looking at the slight circles under her blue-green eyes. They'd left early, too early for her liking, hoping to beat the summer traffic.

School was finally over. Cars, Jeeps, vans, and trucks had choked the highways as students left the Sweet Valley University campus that morning—

heading for homes, beaches, mountains, and airports.

Last night Elizabeth had seen her boyfriend, Tom Watts, off to Colorado, where he was taking an intense three-month communications course. Tom was the anchor and general manager of WSVU, Sweet Valley University's campus television station.

Elizabeth reached into her green canvas backpack sitting on the bed and removed a photo of herself and Tom taken last month at the station. She stuck it in the frame of the mirror. "There," she said. "Now I'm officially moved in."

Jessica appeared in the doorway with an enormous suitcase that looked as if it weighed at least two hundred pounds.

Like Elizabeth, Jessica wore jeans and a cotton tank. But unlike Elizabeth, she wore black patent-leather high-heeled mules with her ensemble. Also unlike Elizabeth, she had rolled her hair that morning in hot rollers and made up her face—complete with eyeliner and a burgundy lip stain.

Elizabeth had scoffed. But she had to admit that Jessica looked a lot better, and a whole lot more glamorous, than she did after the long road trip.

Even though Elizabeth and Jessica were identical twins, no two girls could have been more dissimilar. Elizabeth was a serious student and a committed journalist at the campus news station, who spent very little time thinking about her appearance.

Jessica, on the other hand, had a good brain but

generally hesitated to use it. She coasted through her classes on intelligence and didn't bother to study much. Her grades were acceptable but not impressive.

That didn't bother Jessica at all. She wasn't interested in academics. She was interested in parties, her sorority, men, and fashion. If Jessica had a hobby, it was grooming—which was probably why her suitcase seemed to weigh so much.

Elizabeth knew that Jessica had packed every single toiletry she owned in spite of the fact that Elizabeth had assured her that makeup, shampoo, conditioner, toner, and sunblock could be bought in the shops at Sweet Valley Shore.

Jessica leaned against the door, panting from the exertion of hauling the suitcase. "Wow! Great room. I'll flip you for it."

"Possession is nine-tenths of the law." Elizabeth jumped on the bed and hugged the pillow to her chest. "And I'm in possession."

Jessica frowned. "The two bedrooms on the ground floor are taken. The two bedrooms on this floor are taken. You can't honestly expect—"

Elizabeth pointed upward with her thumb.

"No way. This is unbearable. You mean to tell me that every time I want to go to my room, I'm going to have to go up two flights of stairs!"

"Yup. But think of all the great exercise you'll get. In two weeks you'll have the thinnest thighs on the beach."

"But I already have the thinnest thighs," Jessica said dryly, hoisting her suitcase and taking to the stairs.

Elizabeth went to the window, pushed back the white-dotted curtains, and tied the swags. She heard the ceiling creak and squeak as Jessica explored the top floor. Then she heard the distinct thump of Jessica's heavy suitcase as it dropped directly above her head.

"The other room is occupied," Jessica shouted down the stairs to Elizabeth. "But this room is great. It's bigger than yours."

Elizabeth stepped out on the landing and looked up the stairs. "Really?"

Jessica leaned over the rail above her. "Really. It almost makes up for the extra flight of stairs."

Elizabeth laughed, went back into her own room, and began a close inspection. The closet was narrow, but that was okay. Elizabeth hadn't brought much—some sundresses and a couple of pairs of linen slacks. Everything else was strictly utilitarian. Jeans. Sweaters. T's. Four one-piece bathing suits with heavy-duty straps for lifeguarding. And one not-so-utilitarian sky blue bikini.

Who knew? Maybe Tom would visit Sweet Valley Shore for a weekend. It would be an expensive flight from Colorado, but they'd agreed to arrange at least one visit.

"Hey, Liz . . . do you have my little backpack?" Winston stuck his head in the doorway and looked around.

"Nope."

"Must be in the trunk," Winston said. He sniffed the air. "Doesn't it smell kind of . . . *damp* to you?" he ventured.

"I think that's what's commonly referred to as salt air," Elizabeth said.

He walked over to the window. "I've got the same view downstairs. Don't you feel like the ocean is a little . . . *close*?"

Elizabeth chuckled. She knew Winston was less than enthused at the prospect of spending the summer at Sweet Valley Shore. But his girlfriend, Denise Waters, had gone to Europe for three months. Having no other plan, Winston had agreed to spend his vacation at the beach with Elizabeth, Jessica, Nina, and her boyfriend, Bryan.

Last summer Nina had lived in this same house while she'd worked on the Sweet Valley Shore lifeguard squad. Nina had assured them all that they could get jobs on the squad this summer. It would be like a paid beach vacation.

"All that water makes me nervous," Winston muttered.

Elizabeth laughed. "You'll have to get over that if you plan to be a lifeguard."

Winston's eyebrows rose to his hairline in a parody of dismay. "You mean . . . I might have to *go in*?" Tall and thin, with shaggy chestnut curls, a freckled face, and a bemused expression, Winston resembled a vaudeville comic in his vintage

Bermuda shorts, floppy Hawaiian shirt, and battered white straw fedora.

Elizabeth laughed again, glad that they had convinced him to join them. Winston was hapless, absentminded, an incurable clown, and very entertaining. It was going to be a blast having him around for the summer.

"Got to find that backpack," he said, pushing the brim of the white fedora back with his index finger. "It's got Denise's picture in it. And her number. Not that I can afford to call her yet. I hope Nina was right about being able to get jobs on the squad. I'm pretty close to broke. I already owe Nina the money she lent me for my part of the beach house deposit and the first month's rent."

Winston's usually ironic tone was gone, and his face looked a little tense.

"How did you wind up so far in the hole?" Elizabeth asked.

"Well, I was afraid Denise might forget me in Italy—you know about those incredibly handsome Italian hunks. So I decided to go all out on a going-away present. I bought her a gold bracelet and had it engraved with our initials."

"Winston! How romantic."

"Romantic and expensive," he said. "At any rate, if I don't get a job, I won't be able to pay Nina back or keep up with my share of the expenses."

"Nina knows what she's talking about,"

Elizabeth reassured him. "If she says we can get jobs . . . we can get jobs."

"She also *said* Bryan was coming," Winston reminded her.

"That's a sore subject," Elizabeth said in a warning tone. "Don't say anything about it when we see her. I know she's still upset that Bryan backed out at the last minute. Even though she knows it would have been insane for him to turn down a chance to work on Capitol Hill for the summer."

"At least he found somebody to take his place. Whoever it is, I think he's here. There are a bunch of suitcases in the other downstairs bedroom. They must belong to the mystery roommate. Any idea who it is?"

Elizabeth shook her head. "All Nina said was that he was a friend of Bryan's from high school."

"Hey . . . hey . . . hey!" a familiar female voice shouted from downstairs. "Are you guys here or am I being robbed?"

Elizabeth and Winston hurried out on the landing and looked down.

"Well?" Nina Harper flashed them her famous two-hundred-kilowatt smile. "Was I right about this place or what?"

Nina might have been busy since she arrived, but whatever she'd been doing seemed to agree with her. She looked fabulous. Her dark brown complexion glowed with sunscreen, and a rosy lipstick brought out the color in her cheeks.

10

As usual she wore her dark hair braided. The shoulder-length plaits were studded with bright yellow beads that matched her yellow bathing suit top and shorts. Yellow thongs completed her ensemble, and a pair of running shoes tied together hung from laces over her right shoulder.

Elizabeth hurried down the stairs and threw her arms around her best friend. "You were totally right. This house is incredible. Not that I've had much time to look around."

Nina looked at her watch. "Did you guys just get here?"

"Five minutes ago," Winston confirmed. "Traffic was heavy all the way."

Jessica came thumping down the stairs in her high heels. "Great house, Nina. Where are the rest of our roomies, and when do we get to meet them?"

"They're out on the beach, I guess," Nina said. "And we need to get out there, too. Orientation for lifeguard training starts in twenty minutes."

"Twenty minutes!" Elizabeth, Jessica, and Winston all cried out at once.

"I want to unpack," Jessica said.

"I want to eat," Winston said.

"I want to call Tom," Elizabeth said. "And I want to see the rest of the house."

"Later!" Nina pushed Jessica and Elizabeth up the steps. "Right now it's time to suit up and show up. Let's go. Let's go. Let's *go!*"

*　　*　　*

11

"Hurry up, Jessica!" Nina turned and waved her arms.

Nina, Winston, and Elizabeth walked several yards ahead of Jessica.

"I'm coming," she cried. But she didn't run to catch up. Her feet still hurt from those patent-leather high heels. She'd changed into thongs and a black forties-style two-piece bathing suit, but the backs of her calves felt a bit stiff.

Officially the season wouldn't begin until the Saturday of Memorial Day weekend—a week and a half away. The beach wasn't open for swimming, and there was no one in the water. But the white sand was dotted with colorful beach towels and sunbathers wearing bright swimming trunks, maillots, and bikinis.

The lifeguard station was less than a half mile south of the house. It was a long, wooden one-story building with a wooden walk in the front and a red flag flying from the roof.

Jessica passed a volleyball game in progress and a group of college-age guys working industriously on an elaborate sand castle. The cry of a bird drew her attention to the shoreline. A single white gull swooped down over the heads of a couple standing at the water's edge. White lacy foam lapped at their ankles, and the sun gleamed down on the man's blond hair. Jessica watched as he bent his head over his girlfriend's and kissed her as the wave receded.

A lump rose in Jessica's throat and she quickly

looked away. Summertime meant long days and even longer nights. Interminable nights if you had to spend them alone.

A few moments ago Jessica had felt happy and optimistic. Sure that a new man, a new love, was just around the corner. But seeing the ocean set off a chain of unhappy memories.

Memories of Louis Miles, the young professor with whom she had fallen in love.

Love. She knew what it was like to be in love, all right. And time after time love had left her confused and hurt. *Is love really worth all the pain?* she wondered as she neared the lifeguard station and saw the crowd of young people gathering there.

Louis had lived in a condo on the beach near Sweet Valley University. It had been there that they had shared a few brief, blissful days of happiness before embarking on a terrifying odyssey that ended in Louis's death.

After Louis she had briefly reconnected with her ex-husband, the handsome but destructive Mike McAllery.

"Hey, Blondie, how do I start a conversation with you?"

Jessica looked up, startled. A dark-haired guy with a medium build had fallen into step beside her. He wore red trunks and an oversize white T-shirt. Sunglasses covered most of his face, and he placed the billed University of Chicago baseball cap he'd been carrying low on his forehead, covering his brows.

"You don't," she said curtly, speeding up a little. Her mind was full of Louis and Mike. And she didn't appreciate this guy intruding on her memories.

"Okay. How about you start a conversation with me?"

His voice was deep and casual, with an offhand ironic tone. Jessica wasn't in the mood to score points off some smart aleck with a second-rate body and third-rate material, so she didn't even bother to answer.

"I'm waiting, Blondie."

"Don't call me Blondie," she said in a curt tone, pushing her own sunglasses up on her nose.

"Okay. I'll call you Gorgeous."

"Please leave me alone."

"How can I when I'm hopelessly in love?" He gave the word *love* a particularly sarcastic twist, as if he didn't even believe such a thing existed.

Suddenly all the memories—good and bad—converged, creating a terrible ache in her chest. Jessica's fingers fanned over her diaphragm and pressed in an effort to ease the pain.

Love was real. And she had the scars to prove it. How dare this wise-guy loser trivialize something he didn't even understand?

"Go away," she snarled.

"Whoa!" he said, chuckling at her anger. "Chill out. I'm trying to be friends."

"I've got enough friends," Jessica retorted.

top of his head. An involuntary yawn escaped him.

"Wake up, Winston," Nina teased, poking him in the ribs. "Look alert."

"How can I look alert when my brains are frying inside my head?" He eyed a seat on a nearby lifeguard tower. Farther down the beach several more lifeguard towers were spaced out along the sand. "Aren't those chairs supposed to have umbrellas over them?"

"Of course," she said with a laugh. "They're just not up yet. The beach isn't officially open. But trust me, Winston. No lifeguard has died of sunstroke . . . yet."

Suddenly a tall, thin girl with shoulder-length brown hair ran directly into Winston, knocking him to the ground. She'd been fighting with an out-of-control kite when she'd run into Winston from across the sand. She wore a loose pair of green pants with a drawstring waist and a T-shirt.

"Hey, watch where you're going," Winston said as he stood up and wiped the sand off his pale legs.

"Oh, wow . . . sorry. Are you hurt? I can't believe the summer hasn't even officially started and I'm already getting myself into trouble. Hey, Nina, I didn't even notice you. How are you? I hope your friend here is okay."

"Third-floor beach view, I'd like you to meet first-floor dune and ocean combo." Nina introduced Winston to the girl, then glanced over at the crowd by the station. "Are you okay, Winston? Do you need any help?" Nina reached out and grabbed his elbow.

"Yeah, I'm okay. And I can stand on my own." Winston shrugged out of her grasp.

"Great. Then you won't mind if I leave you here with Wendy. I see a bunch of people I recognize from last year. I'm dying to say hello to them."

"Um . . . well, sure. I'll . . . see you later."

Wendy waved Nina off and reached out to shake Winston's hand. "Nice to meet you. And I do have a name. It's Wendy Wolman. Sorry again for bumping into you like that."

Now that he was standing next to Wendy, Winston couldn't help but notice that she was different from most of the girls he knew. She wasn't unattractive or anything like that. But she wasn't as . . . well . . . *colorful*. No lipstick, mascara, or eyeliner. And she wasn't as curved-in-all-the-right-places.

Still, when she smiled, her gray eyes sparkled and her lightly tanned skin was smooth and flawless.

Winston began to feel better about his prospects. If Wendy, who didn't look terribly athletic, could make it onto the lifeguard squad, then he definitely had a chance.

The crowd of people around the lifeguard station seemed to be growing by the minute. Lots of competition, from the looks of it. Tons. "Who *are* all these people?" Winston asked Wendy. "And why are some of them already wearing lifeguard T-shirts?"

"The people wearing the lifeguard T-shirts are the South Beach Squad. They finished their tryouts last

18

week—not that the results were any big surprise."

"What do you mean?"

Wendy smiled tightly. "South Beach has had pretty much the same cast of characters for the last three years." She pointed. "The tall bombshell with the long dark hair is Rachel Max. She goes to University of Chicago and heads up the South Beach Squad. The African-American guy in the fishing hat is Kyle Fisher. He's her assistant. Henchman is probably a better word."

"Doesn't sound like you're too fond of the South Beach Squad."

"They're snobs. Totally cliquey. Some of them are okay. Mickey Esposito, the short, balding guy, is nice. Kristi Bjorn, too. She's Norwegian." Wendy nodded toward an incredibly pale-skinned girl with long white hair. "Don't ask me how she keeps from burning to a crisp. Oh, and there's Tina Fong, Danielle Dodge, Hunter Pickering, and Jack Fromton. The tall, thin African American girl is new, though. So is the blond guy with the ponytail."

The crowd of people gathered around the lifeguard station began to buzz and stir. Apparently things were about to get started. Winston eyeballed the mob and noted the number of well-built guys. Did he really have a chance? Did he really want one?

"Look. You did this last year, right?" Winston asked.

"Right."

"So what's it like? I mean, if you make it, is it fun? Or is it nerve-racking?"

Wendy pulled down her mouth and mused a moment. "Well," she said after a moment. "If you want to know the truth, it's both. Ryan Taylor heads up the squad. He's tough. He's demanding. And he's not real fair. But he's not afraid of anything that swims, walks, or flies. That makes him a god as far as lifeguards are concerned. Whatever he says, goes. Never argue. And never whine."

Winston forced himself not to execute a 180-degree pirouette and head back for the house. He could do funny. But he couldn't do fearless. And he didn't want to pretend. "I think I may be in over my head," he said. "No pun intended."

"Hey. It's not like Ryan's nuts or anything. He doesn't expect the squad to look death in the face and laugh. He's macho, and I think he permanently lost his sense of humor last summer when—," Wendy broke off.

"When what?"

"Never mind," she said uneasily. "It's a long story." She took his arm and gave it an encouraging squeeze and a shake, as if she wanted to get back to the conversation at hand. "Don't poop out on me," she urged as she pulled him toward the front of the group, where Nina stood with Elizabeth.

Nina dug her toes happily into the sand. So far everything was working out beautifully. Bryan's friend, Ben Mercer, had showed up early this morning with his share of the rent in hand.

The house had been in perfect shape. All the appliances were in good working order. And the gas, water, electricity, and phone had all been hooked up with no delays.

She pictured Bryan's handsome face. Tall and thin, he had a strong build and a quick mind. But sun and surf weren't his thing. Politics was where it was at for Bryan.

Nina stifled the stab of resentment that threatened to spoil an otherwise perfect day. She knew she couldn't expect Bryan to give up an opportunity to work in Washington, D.C., just to hang out with her on the beach. Still, she wished Bryan could cut loose for once and do something ridiculous. Being focused, directed, and motivated was great. Nina was all of those things, too. But she also knew how to relax and have a good time.

A shrill whistle interrupted her thoughts and brought the chattering crowd of people to attention. Ryan Taylor dropped the whistle around his neck, pulled on a T-shirt that said Sweet Valley Shore Lifeguard, and made his way to the center of the crowd. His eyes flickered over the faces gathered around him. When he saw Nina, he smiled briefly and winked his recognition.

"I'm Ryan Taylor. And I'm the head of the Sweet Valley Shore Squad. I've been here the last few years, and I'm glad to see some familiar faces.

Welcome back, Nina. Wendy? Is that you?"

"It's me," she confirmed, peering around Winston. "Glad to see me?" she teased.

"You bet," he said with a nod. "I'm glad to see anybody with some experience."

Nina grinned. Ryan was an intense guy. Complex. Hard to predict. He could make your life a living hell. Or he could totally make your day.

She remembered one particular day last year. At two o'clock he'd chewed Wendy out and summarily fired her for a prank gone wrong. Then at two thirty, when he was finished with his shift, Ryan took Wendy to lunch and drove her around, helping her find another job to finish out the summer.

"As I'm sure you all know," Ryan continued, pitching his voice over the surf and rising wind, "there are five squads. Port Halley Sound. North Sound Squad. Four Mile Beach Squad. Sweet Valley Shore. And South Beach." He held up a piece of paper, which flapped in the breeze. "I'll only be training people for Sweet Valley Shore, so if your name is not on this list, please add it." He attached the piece of paper to a clipboard and circulated it through the crowd.

Nina smiled. She'd done a tremendous job of strategic planning. They had the house. Enough people to cover the cost. And a fun group.

She cut her eyes toward Elizabeth, hoping to exchange a look of triumph at how well things were working out. But Elizabeth was too busy to catch her best friend's stare. Nina saw Elizabeth's glassy gaze glued to Ryan's perfectly chiseled face. *Wow!* Elizabeth seemed to have it bad for the elusive head lifeguard. *Has Elizabeth forgotten about boyfriend Tom before the summer has officially begun?*

"Your *boyfriend* doesn't seem to recognize you," Mr. University of Chicago whispered, sidling up next to Jessica. "Maybe he's got amnesia. Think he hit his head with a surfboard this morning?"

Jessica's eyes narrowed angrily behind her sunglasses. She had been stunned and slightly embarrassed when the incredible hunk she'd pretended was her boyfriend had appeared in the middle of the crowd and introduced himself as head lifeguard Ryan Taylor.

"We don't advertise our relationship," she hissed. "We're trying to keep things professional."

"Ohhh, I see," the guy said with a chuckle, making it obvious he didn't believe her.

Jessica moved several steps away, wishing the creep would have the decency to drown as soon as possible.

Chapter
Three

"Man!" Winston whispered in Elizabeth's ear. "This stuff's pretty intimidating."

"Relax," Elizabeth whispered back. "It sounds harder than it is."

Ryan was describing the drills and training that would take place over the next few days. Elizabeth wasn't worried. She'd been a lifeguard before—at the neighborhood pool when she was in high school. She was a strong swimmer, a fast runner, and a levelheaded person.

Way too levelheaded to develop a crush at first sight on a guy just because he was drop-dead gorgeous and the head of the lifeguard squad.

"I'm not much of a runner," Winston whispered. "Think I can get up to speed in time?"

"Sure," Elizabeth whispered back in a reassuring tone, unable to drag her eyes from Ryan's face. "Nina and I will coach you and—"

"Excuse me!"

Elizabeth broke off when she heard Ryan's sharp, angry tone. She looked around, wondering what had happened to upset him. Then she realized in horror that he was staring right at her.

"If you can't pay attention," he said abruptly, "why don't you just quit now?"

Her heart began a dull, sickening thud. Elizabeth felt utterly humiliated. Completely mortified. And at a total loss as to how to respond.

Nobody had ever spoken to her in that tone before. She was Elizabeth Wakefield. Smart. Responsible. Mature. "I'm sorry," Elizabeth managed to squeak, not knowing what else to say.

"The first thing you're going to have to learn is how to pay attention," Ryan said to everyone. "If you're going to be a lifeguard, you have to pay attention every single minute you're on duty." Then he checked his clipboard, cleared his throat, and continued outlining the drills and training.

"We'll have five days of training starting tomorrow. Then Wednesday, Thursday, and Friday, a break on Saturday, and more training Sunday and Monday. Tryouts will be held on Tuesday. The final squad will have a day to rest and then begin on Thursday and Friday to get used to working together before the beach officially opens the next Saturday. Think you guys can handle that?" He stared directly at Elizabeth, as if he were asking only *her* if *she* could handle it.

25

Mortification turned to anger. Elizabeth's blue-green eyes narrowed. Ryan Taylor's handsome face no longer seemed handsome. It seemed arrogant and rude. Clearly this guy had no idea who he was dealing with. She wasn't some silly child who could be reprimanded in front of the class. If he didn't know that now, he would as soon as the training began. She'd extract an apology from him before it was all over or her name wasn't Elizabeth Wakefield.

Just because the man was handsome, tall, capable, heroic, and had eyes the color of sable didn't mean he could . . .

She stared at his deep brown eyes with tiny flecks of gold and couldn't finish her thought. A smudge of sand on his cheek shone like glitter in the sun and made the amber in his eyes blaze.

Suddenly Elizabeth realized that his intense brown eyes were staring pointedly into hers. "Do you need to take a nap or something?" he asked her in a sharp, impatient tone.

Elizabeth blinked in startled surprise, realizing that once again he was speaking to her.

"Wh-wh-what?" she stammered.

"I asked you a question." His voice sounded slightly less impatient. "But you seem to be asleep."

Elizabeth swallowed. Question? What question? She had no idea what he was talking about . . . or what he had been saying. She'd been staring into his eyes, gazing intently at his face as if she were taking in every word. But not one single thing he'd said had penetrated.

Suddenly the hard line of his lips softened and the corner of his mouth turned up slightly in a half smile. "I know the sun makes people a little spacey sometimes, so everybody try to be realistic about how much heat you can stand. I mean that literally and figuratively. That's it for now. I'll see everybody tomorrow at eight A.M. sharp."

Ryan turned to speak with a tall, sultry young woman with long dark hair. She was wearing a South Beach Lifeguard T-shirt over short blue cutoffs.

The crowd broke up, and a few moments later the sultry young woman walked away to join another lifeguard and a couple of guys who'd resumed their game of Frisbee.

"Wow!" Winston breathed. "He's scary."

"He's . . . he's . . ." Elizabeth was so angry and embarrassed, she didn't know what to say. "I'm going back to the house," she said, mustering all her dignity. "I need to finish unpacking. Come on. We'll jog back together. That'll give you a head start on the training."

Elizabeth stretched her legs a little, preparing to jog down the beach with her head held high. She was a graceful runner and her legs were in good shape. She might have looked like a fool at orientation, but her exit was going to be impressive. "Let's go," she said, breaking into a run.

Winston loped along beside her. But just as she was really breaking into form, her toe caught a piece of driftwood. The next thing she knew, she fell face forward, her body making a loud thud when she hit the wet sand. She heard several people gasp.

"Elizabeth!" Winston's worried voice floated high above her head.

Her ear was against the ground, and she could hear somebody running fast in her direction. A large, firm hand closed over her upper arm, and a strong arm gently reached around her waist. Someone lifted her effortlessly and helped her to her feet.

"I'm okay," she insisted through a mouthful of sand. She opened her eyes and saw a pair of gold-flecked brown eyes inspecting her face, looking for injuries.

One hand firmly held her arm. The other delicately wiped some sand from her eyebrows. When his eyes flickered over the rest of her body, seeming to search for scrapes or cuts, her heart began to hammer and her knees went weak.

"Yup, you're right. You're okay," he confirmed. He released her arm, and she swayed slightly before pulling herself together.

"Be careful," he chided her. "Look where you're going. Like I said, try to be realistic about what you can and *can't* do."

Elizabeth's mouth opened and closed. Once again she was so unaccustomed to being seen as incompetent, she had no idea how to respond. He seemed to read her confusion as spaciness. "Are you *sure* you want to be a lifeguard?" he asked.

28

Elizabeth heard a snort of laughter and looked over just in time to see Jessica turn away with her hand over her mouth.

Jessica pressed a hand to her mouth to keep from bursting into hysterical laughter. She loved her twin sister and she felt sorry for her, but it was pretty funny. For once Elizabeth wasn't being taken seriously. She was getting the kind of treatment Jessica usually got.

"Hey, Blondie! Look out!" There was genuine alarm in the familiar deep voice that shouted the warning.

Jessica instinctively turned her head just as a large white disk whizzed directly toward her head. Instinctively she lifted her hand to protect her face. The rim of the Frisbee connected with her palm, making a loud slap, and she closed her fingers over the rim.

I caught it.

Several people around her began to whistle and clap.

Jessica couldn't believe it. Playing Frisbee had never been her thing. Big, round objects hurtling directly toward her face was about as entertaining as playing with a buzz saw. Not only could you get hurt, you could break a nail.

Now here she was, holding the Frisbee and being applauded like an outfielder who'd just made an impossible catch. Her eyes searched the crowd to see who had thrown it.

A tall, gorgeous brunette in a South Beach Lifeguard T-shirt stood several yards away, staring at Jessica with her hands on her hips. "Sorry," the brunette said in a flat, unapologetic tone. She lifted her hand, indicating that she wanted Jessica to throw the Frisbee back.

Jessica looked around. Where was the University of Chicago guy? He'd been the one who'd shouted the warning. She'd recognized his deep voice.

A pair of bright blue eyes caught her attention. They belonged to a hunk with the most incredible set of abs she'd ever seen. "Watch what you're doing, Rachel," he shouted.

Jessica cocked her head. That was Mr. University of Chicago's voice. But those abs . . . they couldn't be his. Could they? With a shock Jessica recognized the red trunks, sunglasses, and billed baseball cap.

It *was* him. Mr. University of Chicago in the flesh. He'd shed the T-shirt and exposed those killer abs. When he turned his face back toward her, the smart-aleck grin was gone, and he looked genuinely worried.

"Your boyfriend doesn't seem to recognize you." The sneering observation echoed in her memory. Okay. Maybe she was wrong about the second-rate musculature. But he was still obnoxious.

Jessica knew she should thank him for the warning. But she wasn't going to—even if he did have great abs and gorgeous eyes. Jessica set her lips in a grim line and tossed the Frisbee back to the woman who had thrown it. Miraculously it sailed in the right direction. The young woman caught it and turned away without a word of thanks.

"You have good reflexes," another male voice commented.

Jessica turned, and her eyes widened in surprise. Ryan stood beside her with his clipboard under his arm.

"Thanks," she said, tossing her long blond hair off her shoulder, flattered that he was initiating a conversation with her. "Who is that, anyway?"

"Rachel Max. She's the captain of the South Beach Squad." He laughed. "Our arch rivals. She likes to come to my orientation and check out the talent. See what the competition looks like. I hope you're trying out for the squad and not just sightseeing."

"I am." She gave him her most dazzling smile. The one that had been known to freeze men in their tracks. She widened her eyes slightly so the dark fringe of her lashes practically touched her brow bone. Jessica's delicately tinted pink lips stretched into a wide smile that showed both rows of perfect white teeth.

But Ryan didn't freeze in his tracks, swallow convulsively, or even blush. None of the usual reactions.

Instead he cocked his head, stared at her, then turned back toward the shoreline where Elizabeth had fallen. He squinted, his mind working. "Wait a minute . . ."

"We're twins," Jessica explained. "Identical

twins. I'm Jessica Wakefield. And that was my sister, Elizabeth, who fell down."

Ryan smiled and nodded. "Whew, I thought the sun was getting to me and I was seeing double."

Jessica laughed and cast a sideways look at him. He made no move to walk away and didn't appear to be in a hurry to terminate the conversation. Jessica took that as an encouraging sign.

When Ryan made no further remark, she realized it was up to her to keep the conversational ball rolling. She could talk about being twins, but since Elizabeth wasn't making a favorable impression, maybe it was better to think of something else.

"We're roommates with Nina Harper," she informed him brightly, pleased to have come up with a friendship with someone who reflected a little more glory than her sister.

"Oh, that's great. The Krebbs place is a terrific house. Who else is there this summer?" he asked.

"Nina made all the arrangements," she said. "And I haven't met two of the people yet, but—" She broke off when she noticed Mr. University of Chicago watching her and Ryan.

Determined to prove Ryan was her boyfriend, Jessica smiled her dazzling smile again, put her right hand on Ryan's arm, and leaned a little closer. The gesture was rather intimate, and his face registered slight surprise. But he didn't withdraw the arm. And he didn't look displeased.

"Thanks for helping my sister," she said sweetly.

His rugged face broke into a smile. "Anytime," he assured her gently. "That's what I'm here for."

"Hey, Ryan! May I speak with you?" A policeman in a broad-rimmed straw hat waved his arm. Behind him, parked on the beach, was a white GMC truck with an extended cab. Sheriff's Department was stenciled on the side in bright red letters.

"I'm sorry, but I've got to go," Ryan said. "That's Captain Feehan. He keeps an eye on Sweet Valley Shore and South Beach. You'll be seeing a lot of him once you start work." He smiled, resting his hand briefly on top of Jessica's. It felt warm, slightly calloused, and intriguingly masculine. "So I'll see you tomorrow."

He lifted his hand, and Jessica let her own soft hand slide slowly off his broad forearm. "See you tomorrow," she confirmed.

Ryan jogged off toward the truck, and Jessica searched the thinning crowd for Mr. University of Chicago. When she found him, she smiled smugly. It took a lot of self-control not to triumphantly stick out her tongue at him.

Chapter Four

"Watch it. That's hot stuff . . . ," Winston warned as Nina grabbed the Pyrex dish full of asparagus off the counter.

"Yeoowww!" Nina yelped. She dropped the dish and it fell to the floor with a crash.

"I tried to warn you," Winston said, carefully removing a pot of boiling pasta from the back burner.

Winston had nominated himself master chef for the evening, and with the "help" of his roommates, he was attempting to put together a dinner of shrimp, pasta, green salad, asparagus, and garlic bread.

Elizabeth stood at the sink, peeling shrimp and staring out the single kitchen window. Ever since her fall, she'd seemed discouraged, distracted, and irritable.

Nina bumped her aside with her hip and put her burned hands under the faucet.

"Why don't you do that in the bathroom?" Elizabeth suggested in a tight voice.

"Because my hands hurt here and now," Nina answered.

"I'm ready for a break anyway," Elizabeth said glumly, wiping her hands on a towel. She pulled a red ladder-back chair away from the wooden table with a loud squeak.

"I'll take over," Wendy offered, pushing up the sleeves of her green sweatshirt and reaching for a shrimp. Her long dark hair was caught back in a ponytail and a wildflower was tucked festively into the rubber band.

The kitchen was small but well equipped with an oven, a microwave, and a good-sized refrigerator. The floors were red-and-black parquet. The walls were white, with a green-and-red stencil pattern around the ceiling. A green wire spice rack had been mounted on the wall next to the oven.

It reminded Winston of his grandmother's kitchen, and for the first time since orientation he began to feel at home and cheerful.

"Coming through. Coming through," Jessica announced, walking through the swinging door that separated the kitchen from the living room. Everyone else wore the bathing suits, shorts, and T-shirts they had worn that afternoon, but Jessica had changed into a pink halter sundress.

"Look out," Winston warned, skirting around her. Holding the large pasta pot with two oven mitts, he put the pot down on a plastic sheet that protected the Formica countertop from scorches. "Hey, Jess, would you please get me the butter?" Winston asked.

"Sorry. My nails are wet."

"Elizabeth?" Winston asked. "Could you reach into the fridge and hand me the butter?"

Elizabeth settled her chin more firmly on her fist and stared glumly at the wall.

"Elizabeth!" Winston prompted.

The refrigerator door was right behind Elizabeth. She didn't even have to stand in order to open the door and reach the butter. But instead of jumping up to get it, she let out a long, suffering sigh. Winston wasn't the only one who'd returned from orientation less than enthused. And the kitchen didn't seem to be having the same cheering effect on Elizabeth that it was having on him.

"Would you please quit sulking," Nina begged. She shook the water off her hands and then set about picking up the shards of broken Pyrex and dropped food. She threw a handful of asparagus into the garbage. "And would you knock off the moaning and groaning? It's very un-you."

Nina went over to the refrigerator and rummaged through the shelves of groceries that the group had purchased that afternoon. Butter. Milk. Yogurt. Cheese. Six kinds of cereal. Berries of every description. And vegetables.

"I can't help it." Elizabeth sighed again. "I feel like an idiot."

Nina removed the butter and a couple of tomatoes. "You got off to a bad start," she told Elizabeth. "But nobody's going to remember anything by tomorrow. They'll be too busy thinking about the drills and the tryouts."

Elizabeth simply groaned again and closed her eyes as if nothing anybody said would make her feel better. "I've never been so embarrassed in my whole life. I can't go back there tomorrow."

Jessica sat down at the table across from Elizabeth and giggled. "You're not setting a very good example," she teased.

"For who?"

"For any of us."

"Nina's right," Winston said, putting a hand on Elizabeth's shoulder. "Like it or not, we all look up to you. If you let us down by weaking out at the first setback, what's left for us to believe in?"

Everybody laughed, and even Elizabeth cracked a reluctant smile. "Easy for you to say," she commented. "You didn't make a fool out of yourself."

"*Yet,*" Winston corrected. He trailed his fingers along the matching spice jars until he found what he was looking for. The garlic. He removed the cap and prepared to sprinkle it over the pan of bread waiting to be heated in the oven.

Jessica stood at his elbow with her fingers still spread. "No garlic," she said gently.

"No garlic!" Winston protested. "How can you have garlic bread without garlic?"

"I don't want to have bad breath tomorrow," Jessica explained.

"But . . ."

Jessica got up, delicately took the garlic jar from his hand, and threw it out the window. "No garlic," she repeated with a serene smile. Then she sat back down across from her sister and resumed blowing on her nails.

"She's right," Nina said. "There are way too many hunks out there on the beach. We don't want to get a reputation as the girls who stink."

Winston rolled his eyes. "This is as bad as living in my dorm."

Nina, Jessica, and Elizabeth laughed at the thought of Winston back at Sweet Valley University.

Wendy looked confused. "Huh?"

"Due to a bureaucratic snafu, Winston is the only male resident in an all-girl dorm," Nina explained to Wendy.

"Wow! That must be a blast," Wendy said with a wink.

Winston opened the oven door and slid the pan of bread in. "It has been fun. And if it hadn't happened, I might never have met Denise, the light and love of my life. But believe me, I know a whole lot more about exfoliating and deep-pore cleansing than I ever wanted to." He closed the door and adjusted the temperature. "Don't get me wrong. I like female company. But I'd hoped I wouldn't be the only guy in the house this summer."

"You won't feel so outnumbered when Ben gets here," Nina said.

"So where is the mystery roomie, anyway?" Jessica asked.

Bryan's friend, Ben Mercer, hadn't yet made an appearance. So far the only person who'd met him was Nina.

Right on cue, there was a rumble in the living room as the screen door and heavy front door both slammed shut. "Hello?" a deep voice shouted. "Is anybody home?"

"In here," everybody chorused.

The kitchen door swung open and a guy walked in wearing red trunks, a large T-shirt, sunglasses hanging from his neck, and a University of Chicago baseball cap. "Hi," he said with a smile. He seemed to look directly at Jessica as she continued to blow on her wet nails. "This must be my lucky day."

Jessica's heart gave a sickening thump and she froze in midblow, with her cheeks puffed out like a chipmunk's.

Nina jumped up and took his sleeve. "Ben, come in and meet your roomies."

Mr. University of Chicago's eyes crinkled in an amused smile as he looked at Jessica. He reached out his hand to shake hers. "We've met, but we haven't been formally introduced. How do you do? I'm Ben Mercer."

Jessica realized she had all ten fingers spread out and that the pink polish was still sticky. She wiggled her hands to indicate that her nails were wet and thus was spared the obligation of shaking his hand.

Ben continued to stare at her, clearly expecting her to introduce herself. She racked her brains for some cutting remark and came up blank. "Jessica Wakefield," she said in a clipped voice, forced to settle for being rude.

Nina shot her a puzzled look. But Ben didn't even seem to notice as he turned to shake hands with Elizabeth, Wendy, and Winston.

"I looked for you after orientation," Nina said. "Where did you go?"

"I went to Hamburger Harry's—on the pier between Sweet Valley Shore and South Beach. It's a great spot."

While the group chatted and traded notes on where to go and what to do, Jessica felt her heart sink down into her shoes. This was awful. Of all the millions of guys in the world that Bryan could have gotten to take his place—why did it have to be this loser?

"Wow!" Ben was looking back and forth between

Elizabeth's face and Jessica's. "Nina said you two were identical. But I've never seen two people who looked more alike." He craned his neck and peered at Elizabeth's hands. "Uh-oh. There's a continuity problem. You're not wearing any nail polish."

"What's wrong with nail polish?" Jessica demanded, sounding more hostile and antagonistic than she'd intended to.

Ben removed his baseball hat and his brows flew up to his dark hairline. "Not a thing. I'm a pink man myself." He gave her pink dress a pointed look.

Jessica immediately revised her wardrobe plan for tomorrow, deciding to wear the yellow bathing suit instead of her pink one. She didn't want this guy to get the impression she was dressing to please him.

Ben's blue eyes were disturbingly penetrating, and his crooked smile made Jessica feel as if he were reading her mind and laughing at her thoughts. She forced the picture of his etched stomach muscles to the back of her mind. If Ben did have some weird power to read minds, she didn't want him to think she thought he was cute or anything like that.

Jessica lowered her eyes and fidgeted with her nails, wiping a smudge from the corner of one cuticle.

"So, does your boyfriend like pink, too?" Ben

asked, straddling the chair beside her. A pile of large green pottery plates was stacked in the center of the table, along with green paper napkins and utensils. Ben began automatically arranging them, reaching out to set a place in front of each chair.

"What boyfriend?" Elizabeth, Nina, and Winston exclaimed in one voice.

Jessica wished she could kick them all.

"Ryan Taylor," Ben said. "He's Jessica's boyfriend. Right?" His face looked completely innocent, but Jessica could tell he was deliberately trying to embarrass her.

Nina laughed. "Who in the world told you that?"

Ben carefully placed a napkin and fork at Jessica's elbow. "Somebody on the beach," he answered.

Jessica looked up at him and he winked.

She didn't wink back. In fact, she didn't even smile. She lowered her eyelids provocatively and fixed Ben with a level stare. "Ryan Taylor may not be my boyfriend now. But he will be by the end of the week," she announced. Then she inhaled deeply and blew haughtily on her fingernails as her housemates began a good-natured round of teasing.

"That's Jenny Sinclair's condo up there." Wendy pointed toward a brightly lit beach house. She and Winston were walking off the heavy dinner they had eaten by taking a nighttime tour of Sweet Valley Shore's celebrity beach houses. It was a cool evening, and they had changed from shorts into jeans and boots with thick socks.

"Jenny Sinclair! Wow! I love Jenny Sinclair. Have you seen her around here?"

"I've seen her going into the hair salon," Wendy said. "She goes about three times a week."

"Whose house is that?" Winston asked. He pointed to a structure that looked more like a Tudor-style castle than a beach house.

"Pat MacGuire's house."

"*The* Pat MacGuire?" Winston breathed.

"Yeah. But he's never there. I've been life-guarding at Sweet Valley Shore for three summers and I've never seen him or his wife. Just the caretaker. A lot of famous people have full-time caretakers."

"Wow! I had no idea Sweet Valley Shore was so glamorous."

Wendy smiled, gratified by Winston's enthusiasm. After a while most people at the shore took the occasional celebrity appearance pretty much for granted. But for Wendy it was a thrill every time she saw a famous face. She was totally star-struck.

They were walking along Dune Boulevard, a mile-long winding road lined with expensive homes. Here and there a cul-de-sac had been completely landscaped, and some of the houses

43

even appeared to have backyards with grass and flower beds.

Dune Boulevard wasn't the only celebrity-studded residential street. Lookout Road and Ocean Place also featured many luminaries among their residents.

"How do you know about all these stars?" Winston asked. "We've walked at least four miles through town and you've pointed out twenty different celebrity houses. Some of them are famous for being reclusive. How do you know where they live?"

"Well," Wendy said, "I'll tell you if you promise not to rat on me."

"I promise."

"Lifeguards have to fill out a weekly report at the police station. Whenever I'm there, I flip through the computer residential files and see if there are any famous names listed."

"Aha!"

"Good thing I'm not a deranged stalker, huh?"

"I'll say."

"That's how I found out where my fave—Pedro Paloma—lives. Which is right . . . there." They paused outside a two-story house with a yard surrounded by a fence. A light was on over the door, but the rest of the house was dark.

"Wow! I love listening to Pedro Paloma's stuff. He's such a great singer. Too bad he doesn't seem to be home right now," Winston said.

"I *know* he's not home. He's singing at the Sand Bar down at the pier tonight. That's our next stop. Unless you're too pooped."

"Who me? Pooped?" Winston smiled. "I'm never pooped. Denise says I'm unpoopable. So let's boogie on to the Sand Bar." He offered Wendy his arm, and she slipped hers companionably through his.

Wendy studied his profile. Winston wasn't handsome. At least not like most of the hunky guys around the beach. But he was good-looking in an offbeat way. He was tall, with thick, shaggy chestnut-colored curls. He was sweet. And he'd mentioned his girlfriend Denise's name about fifty times since she'd met him that afternoon.

"I'm glad you're madly in love with Denise," Wendy admitted.

"Why is that?"

"Because now I'll have somebody to hang with. Last year everybody was coupled off by about week two. I was the only single person in the house. In fact, I think I was the only single person on the beach. Maybe the only single person in all of California."

The paved road turned to blacktop along a curve, and they stepped carefully through the tall grass that sprouted along the shoulder. "Yeah," Winston answered. "But you'll probably fall for some guy tomorrow afternoon and then *I* won't have anybody to hang with. In fact, I'm surprised they're not lining up outside the house for you."

Wendy pulled Winston to a stop and let go of his arm. A breeze from the direction of the ocean lifted the tendrils of hair around her forehead and tickled her face. She shivered slightly and pulled the sleeves of her sweatshirt down so that they covered her arms.

"Look. You're a really nice guy, but there's something you should know about me. I hate when people pretend I'm something I'm not. I know I'm a plain Jane. And to tell you the truth, it doesn't bother me. If I'd been born good-looking, I might not have developed my winning sense of humor. The way I see it, you can only date so long. But you can laugh all your life."

"I don't get it. What are you trying to say?"

"I'm saying I'm okay with my looks and I'm okay with not having a boyfriend. To tell you the truth, my preferred brand of reality is fantasy. I'd rather sit behind the Sand Bar and dream about Pedro Paloma than spend the evening with somebody I'm not really interested in."

"Well, thanks a lot," Winston responded in a comic huff.

"You know what I mean." She put her arm through Winston's, and they continued in the direction of the Sand Bar. "Winston! What are you doing?" She screamed and jumped straight up in the air when something wet snuffled at the back of her leg.

"Nothing, I swear."

"I just felt something wet on my leg." Wendy's eyes focused in the dark, and she saw a large shaggy dog retreating against the fence. "Hello there," she said in a kind voice.

The dog looked uncertain.

She stooped down and held out her hand. His tail wagged halfheartedly, and after a moment's deliberation the dog inched forward and gave her fingers a tentative sniff.

"Think he's lost?" Winston asked.

Wendy coaxed the dog into the glow of the streetlight. His coat was dirty and matted. Filthy, actually, and about five different colors. "No collar," she muttered. "And there's a lot of rib under here. I'll bet he's a stray. It's so sad when people dump dogs they don't want out here."

While Wendy's fingers searched the dirty fur of his neck again to double check, he let out a little whimper and rolled his big brown eyes up at her face.

"Did you ever see such a gorgeous pair of eyes?" she asked, feeling a warm, melting sensation around her heart.

"They look like Pedro Paloma's," Winston commented.

"I know. And I think I'm in love. Give me your belt." Winston removed his braided belt from his jeans and handed it to her. Wendy looped it around the dog's neck and made a leash. When she had it securely fastened, she leaned over and kissed the mutt on the nose. "I hereby name you Paloma Perro, in honor of the only man in the world with eyes as beautiful as yours."

Paloma Perro lifted his head and snuffled her face affectionately. Wendy gave him a pat. "He's really thin. Let's take him back to the house and find him something to eat. I'll bet he's starved."

"Are you kidding? And miss the concert?" Winston dug down into his pockets and produced a five-dollar bill. "Hot Dog Howie's stand is on the same block as the Sand Bar. Let's get three hot dogs, sit behind the Sand Bar, and catch the end of Pedro Paloma's concert."

Wendy grinned. "Perfect! A romantic evening for three." She leaned over and kissed Paloma Perro on the nose again.

Winston reached over to pat him. But instead of giving Winston's hand a sniff, Paloma lifted his lip in a snarl.

"Paloma!" Wendy admonished, tugging on the leash belt. The dog lowered his ears and tail but continued to glare at Winston.

Winston held up his hands and backed a step or two away. "Okay! Okay! She's your date. No argument."

Wendy laughed. "Be polite, Paloma. We've got the whole summer to be alone together."

Chapter
Five

Elizabeth heard the springs of Jessica's bed groan from the room above her head. Jessica's heels struck the floorboards with a sense of purpose as she scurried from one side of the room to the other.

When Jessica turned on the sink in the upstairs bathroom, the pipes in the wall began to sing. A few moments later Jessica turned off the water and stumped back into her room.

Elizabeth heard the faint slam of the closet door, followed by the squeak of bureau drawers being opened and shut.

Groaning, Elizabeth turned over in her own bed and looked at the clock. It wasn't even six thirty in the morning. *What's Jessica doing up at this hour? I hope nothing's wrong.*

Elizabeth pushed back her cotton quilt and got out of bed. She shoved her feet into the slip-on Keds she used as slippers to protect her feet from the sheen of sand that was always on the floor.

It was a chilly morning, and Elizabeth shivered in the long red Sweet Valley University T-shirt she used as a nightgown. Quietly, to avoid disturbing Nina, who was asleep in the room across the hall, Elizabeth left her room and climbed the stairs to the converted attic that formed the third-floor bedrooms.

Jessica's bedroom door was open, and she lay on the floor with her feet tucked under the footboard of the bed and her arms folded behind her head.

"Twenty-three . . . four . . . five . . . ," she counted as she executed a series of sit-ups. Jessica was dressed in a fire-engine red leotard.

"Am I dreaming?"

"Nope," Jessica puffed.

"What are you doing?"

"I'm getting in shape."

"I don't think you're going to improve your shape much by eight o'clock," Elizabeth teased.

"I'll be in better shape than you are," Jessica challenged. "I'm already in better shape than you are."

"In your dreams," Elizabeth countered.

"I am," Jessica insisted. "Look at you. You're so tired and worn out, you can hardly stand up straight. Whereas I am up and at 'em. I've just finished twenty-five sit-ups."

"What's going on in here?" Wendy asked sleepily, appearing in the doorway. She was wearing a man's long flannel shirt and big fuzzy slippers.

"Jessica is just doing a little pretraining training," Elizabeth explained.

"Not a bad idea," Wendy said. "I think I'll go for a jog."

"See," Jessica said as Wendy disappeared back into her own room. "I'm inspiring everybody. Come on. Do some push-ups with me."

Elizabeth groaned. "It's too early."

"Come on, Liz. You spent way too much time sitting in front of your computer over the last month. You're in terrible shape."

"Stop saying that. I am not."

"You are, too. You couldn't even jog down the beach without falling flat on your face."

Elizabeth's eyes narrowed. "Jessica," she said in a warning tone.

Jessica pursed her lips before answering. "Twenty push-ups and I won't ever mention it again."

"Promise?"

"Promise."

Elizabeth groaned again, got down on the floor, and placed her hands on the ground in front of her. "You do the counting," she said.

"One," Jessica began.

By push-up number ten, Elizabeth realized Jessica was right. The last few weeks had been grueling. Exams. Papers. Last-minute stuff to do at the station. In the middle of all that craziness there had been little time for exercise.

There hadn't been much time for *anything*, including Tom.

Elizabeth and Tom had hardly seen each other in all the end-of-the-year rush.

When they'd kissed good-bye at the airport, it had been hasty and stiff. As if they'd spent so much time apart, they'd forgotten how to feel comfortable with each other.

How had that happened?

Is Tom bored? she wondered. And if so, would he find somebody in Colorado?

Elizabeth pushed the thought out of her mind and redoubled her efforts. Her arms were shaking by the time Jessica counted off fifteen. At push-up number eighteen, she threw in the towel and collapsed on the floor.

Beads of sweat soaked her hairline. "I'm through," she panted, lumbering to her feet. "I'm going downstairs to take a shower."

"Okay," Jessica chirped, finishing push-up number twenty. She hopped up. "I'll take one, too, and meet you in the kitchen in ten minutes."

Elizabeth hurried down to her own room, grabbed her towel, and ducked into the bathroom. Across the hall she could hear Nina stirring.

By the time Elizabeth emerged from the bathroom, Nina was standing outside, waiting to go in. "Good morning," she said, giving Elizabeth a sleepy but bright smile. "Ready for some heavy-duty lifeguard training?"

52

"No, actually. But I will be," she promised.

Nina went in and shut the door, and Elizabeth hurried into her room. She rummaged in a drawer and pulled on the navy blue maillot that had been folded at the bottom. In a matter of seconds she had added a pair of track shorts, a Hawaiian shirt, a visor, sunblock, and thongs.

Dressed and ready to go in two minutes flat.

Beach life was good, she decided, beginning to feel better now that she'd had a shower and coffee was only moments away.

Elizabeth heard the bathroom door open. Nina stumped across the landing to her room.

"I'm going down," Elizabeth called out.

"Don't eat all the doughnuts," Nina shouted back.

Jessica came thumping down the stairs, wearing a yellow T-strap suit with high-cut legs. No cover-up. Her hair was caught in a banana clip and an artfully tousled ponytail cascaded from her crown. Instead of thongs she wore patent-leather beach shoes with a one-inch wedge, creating the glamorous look of high heels. Over her shoulder she carried an enormous canvas bag. "Did I hear somebody say we have doughnuts? Great. I think I can afford one after my morning workout."

"Brag, brag, brag," Elizabeth teased.

Downstairs they found Ben awake, dressed in bathing trunks and a T-shirt. He was hovering outside the kitchen door. "Uh . . . there seems to be a problem in the kitchen."

"What kind of a problem?" Elizabeth asked.

Ben opened the door a few inches so they could peer in.

Elizabeth and Jessica looked inside and then jumped back when a large shaggy dog lunged toward the door, barking ferociously.

Ben let the door close.

"Where did *that* come from?" Jessica squeaked.

Ben opened his hands. "He was in there when I got up. And he doesn't seem to want to let me in."

"What's going on?" Nina appeared, dressed again in her yellow suit and shorts, her braids wet from the shower.

Elizabeth opened the door and let Nina see for herself. A loud, ominous growl indicated that the dog didn't like Nina's looks any more than he'd liked theirs.

"Winston!" Nina shouted.

There was no answer.

Nina walked down the hall to the dining room, which had been converted into a bedroom, and knocked on the door. "Winston? Winston, are you awake?"

After a long pause the door opened and Winston appeared. He wore vintage silk pajama bottoms, no shirt, and had white pimple medicine dotted on his forehead and chin. "What's wrong?" he asked groggily.

"*A*—it's time to wake up. *B*—there's a dog in the kitchen."

"Oh. That's Paloma." Winston yawned.

"Paloma?"

"Yeah. He's a stray. Wendy and I found him last night. She named him after the singer Pedro Paloma. Dogs are cool, right? I mean, there's no antipet clause in the lease or anything like that, is there?"

"We're cool with him," Elizabeth explained. "He's just not cool with us."

"Huh?"

"He won't let us in the kitchen."

Winston walked down the hall, put his hand on the swinging kitchen door, and pushed it open a few inches. "Paloma?" he said in a friendly voice.

His greeting was answered with a volley of barks and growls. Winston pushed the door open a few more inches. "Paloma, it's me, Winston. Remember? The guy who bought you a hot dog last night?" He started to step into the kitchen, but the snarls became so menacing, he quickly changed his mind.

Winston let the door swing shut. "I guess he's not a morning person."

Nina looked at her watch. "Winston, you've got to do something. We're supposed to be at the lifeguard station at eight. We need to eat."

"I guess we'll just have to wait for Wendy to get back," Winston said. "In the meantime I'll put on my suit."

Elizabeth went into the living room and sat down on the big sofa. It was covered in a broad magenta-and-white-striped canvas. The cushions were heavy and made a dull, thudding sound when she flopped on them. She could hear the ocean outside, and the damp morning chill hovered in the high-ceilinged room.

"I hope she gets back soon," Ben said, heading to his room. "I'm starving."

Curiously, Elizabeth had no appetite, even after her miniworkout. Maybe it was the anticipation. Or maybe it was fear. Fear of looking like a fool in front of Ryan.

Why do I care what he thinks? she wondered angrily.

And why was she so bugged by the fact that Jessica looked positively drop-dead fabulous?

Jessica ducked into the downstairs bathroom that Ben and Winston shared. As long as she had a few extra minutes, she might as well put them to good use. She put her canvas bag on the black-and-white tile floor and removed her comb, her hair spray, her waterproof mascara, and her foundation with sunscreen.

A steady churning sound emanated from the toilet tank and Jessica jiggled the handle, trying to stop the flow of water. When the sound didn't abate, she gave up. Toilets were a guy thing. Ben and Winston could worry about it. She had more important things on her mind.

She'd slept heavily and dreamed happily of Ryan. Nonetheless, there was a little puffiness around her eye area. She dabbed gently at it with her concealer and examined the results in the mirror with a critical eye.

"I look like a raccoon," she muttered irritably, reaching for a piece of toilet paper to buff down the circular white rings she had inadvertently created.

"Ahem!"

In the mirror Jessica saw Ben leaning against the doorjamb, watching her with a gleam of a amusement in his eyes. "Are you getting ready for a beauty contest or lifeguard training?"

She ignored him and coolly reached for her comb. She'd grown up with an older brother, so she knew how to handle a pain-in-the-neck guy. Long years of experience had taught her that the best way to deal with male needling was to ignore it. There was nothing wrong with wanting to look her best. Why get defensive?

She poked at her ponytail with the end of the teasing comb as if to say, *Who cares what you think?*

"Brrrrr," he joked. "It's almost as chilly in here as it is on the North Pole."

"Then take the hint and split," she advised tonelessly.

"If anybody's going to split, it's you. You have a bathroom on the third floor, and I need to get in here and take a shower."

Jessica lowered the comb.

Unfortunately he had her on that one. According to the unofficial house rules, this bathroom was Winston and Ben's. Other people could use it when they were on the first floor, but Ben and Winston had seniority. And the need for a shower outranked the need for a primp.

Without haste she dropped her comb, concealer, and spray into the bag. "I'm finished anyway."

He picked up the lipstick she'd left on the rim of the white porcelain sink. "Are all the girls at Sweet Valley University like you?"

"Nope. I'm one of a kind. Are all the men at University of Chicago like you?" she shot back, brushing past him.

"No," he said. "Most of them aren't as smart. Did I mention I'm in Mensa?"

"What's Mensa?" she asked, feeling the first flicker of serious interest in her obnoxious housemate. "A fraternity?"

He let out a snort. "No. It's not a fraternity. It's an organization for people with genius IQs."

She stared at him, trying to decide if he was pulling her leg. "You're a genius?" she asked in a skeptical tone.

"That's what they tell me," he gloated, taking a step closer. They were inches apart now, and his blue eyes were sparkling. Ben seemed happy to have finally engaged her in a conversation.

Jessica reached up and twirled her ponytail. "So tell me something, Ben," she purred through pouting lips.

"Anything," he said, responding immediately to her provocative manner.

"If you're so smart, how come you can't figure out I'm not interested in you?"

His face fell slightly. His eager, interested face closed up and took on a heavy-lidded, sarcastic expression. "Maybe you're just not smart enough to know a good thing when you see it."

"I saw it," she said. "And his name is Ryan Taylor." She strolled out of the bathroom with her hips swaying.

"Want to know a secret?" he asked, reaching for the knob of the bathroom door.

Curious, she turned.

"That bathing suit makes you look fat," he whispered before closing the door with a decisive bang.

That did it. Jessica's cool composure went out the window. She turned and kicked the door. Inside, she heard him laughing as he climbed into the shower and turned on the water.

Jessica went running up the steps with her carryall. Ben might be needling her. But on the other hand, the legs on her yellow suit *were* a little revealing. Maybe her thighs didn't look as good as she thought they did.

There was a black suit in her bottom drawer. The legs were cut lower, but the sides and straps were connected with brass rings. It covered a multitude of sins and was a real eye-catcher.

She'd caught Ryan's eye yesterday, and she wanted to catch it again today. Catch it. Keep it. And rub Ben's sarcastic pointy nose in the fact.

Chapter Six

"Nina, I'm hereby appointing you assistant head lifeguard of the Sweet Valley Shore Squad." Ryan thrust the clipboard with everybody's forms and applications into her hand.

Nina smiled, honored that Ryan trusted her enough to make her his assistant. He obviously had a lot of faith in her and was absolutely certain she'd complete the training and qualify in the tryouts.

The crowd of potential lifeguards had shrunk dramatically from the day before. Still, there was heavy competition—about forty women and men who seemed to be in superb shape.

Nina knew from experience that the pool of candidates would get smaller each day. The grueling drills tended to ruthlessly shrink their numbers.

She felt a thump of worry. Would all her housemates make the squad? And if they didn't, would it cause problems?

60

She glanced at Jessica and Elizabeth, standing side by side. At Wendy, Ben, and Winston. They were here this summer to have a good time. But they were here to work, too.

Nina made up her mind that one way or the other, they were all going to make the squad. Even if it killed them. And her.

Ryan pulled his lifeguard T-shirt off and pointed to a platform anchored in the water. "There's a light surf today. And the current is mild. Let's loosen up with a quarter-mile swim. Out to the platform and back." He tugged on the stretchy neck strap of his goggles, loosening it so that he could put them on.

Nina nervously cleared her throat. "Um . . . Ryan," she said. "I can't swim yet. Neither can Jessica, Elizabeth, Ben, Wendy, or Winston."

Ryan paused. "Why not?"

"We had a problem with a dog," she said.

"One dog bit six people? That sounds more like a bear than a dog."

Everybody laughed when Nina explained that because the dog had kept them from entering the kitchen, breakfast had been delayed by almost half an hour. They had just finished their meal minutes before reporting to the beach. It was too soon for them to attempt a swim.

Ryan's lips had disappeared and the muscle in his jaw pulsed like a metronome.

Uh-oh! Nina thought. She knew Ryan well

enough to know when he was severely peeved. She braced herself.

Ryan lowered his goggles. "Let's get something straight, people. I don't care about problems with dogs. I don't care about problems with cars. Parents. Kids. Whatever. Schedule your meals so that you can swim. Visitors out here on the beach are depending on you to save their lives. If you show up and you can't swim, you can't do the job. And you're not going to do them, or me, any good at all. Let's see some hands. Who *can* swim?"

Elizabeth raised her hand. "I can swim," she said. "I didn't eat breakfast."

Ryan thrust his tongue into his cheek, and Nina closed her eyes. *Big mistake, Elizabeth!*

Nina also knew Ryan's peeves. And Elizabeth had just inadvertently hit one.

"Not eating before you come to the beach is like forgetting to put gas in your car before you start on a trip. If you don't eat, you will run out of gas. This is basic nutrition information. I would think that anybody smart enough to get into college would know that. Please, people, don't waste my time or yours. Why should I trust you to take care of somebody else if you can't take care of yourself?"

Nina watched Elizabeth's face register the same kind of shock and embarrassment she had experienced the day before. Her mouth fell open and her face turned beet red.

"Okay." Ryan sighed. He motioned the group to sit down. "We'll swim later and go over hazards and topography now. It's important that you understand the structure of the bottom, the holes, the currents, and where the rock outcroppings are. And pay attention," he advised sternly, looking right at Elizabeth. "Because there *will* be a written test on this before the tryouts."

Elizabeth's blue-green eyes appealed to Nina for support. But Nina dropped her eyes, avoiding the obvious plea for help.

Elizabeth Wakefield was the most responsible person Nina knew. And Ryan was being overly harsh. But he was right about what he was saying. Making an example of Elizabeth today might save a life tomorrow.

It wasn't fair. But the ocean didn't play fair.

Life and death wasn't a board game. It was literally life and death. They'd found that out last summer. . . .

Nobody's feelings were more important than saving lives. Nobody's friendship, either.

Two hours later Winston flopped down on the sand. The muscles in his arms and legs felt like rubber.

The group had just completed the quarter-mile swim. Winston had wanted to start back about halfway out, but Nina wouldn't let him. In fact, she'd threatened to push him under and drown him if he didn't complete the swim.

Winston threw a wary glance over his shoulder. Ryan scared him to death. And Nina was getting tougher by the hour. She was beginning to sound just like Ryan when she gave instructions.

He glanced around at the muscular bodies that were arranging themselves on the sand, getting ready to do sit-ups and push-ups. Nobody else even looked winded from the swim.

A towel dropped over his face. "Hey!" he cried.

The towel came away, and Wendy smiled down at him. "How are you doing?" She flopped down beside him. Wendy's body looked deceptively frail. She was slender, but in her suit and covered with sunblock Winston could see the well-defined muscles in her long arms and legs.

"I'm not doing too well," he admitted. "I had no idea this was going to be so hard. My muscles are tired. My brain is tired. And this is just day one."

"Everybody feels like that on day one," Wendy reassured him.

Winston stared gloomily out over the water. "If I don't get a lifeguard job, I'm in major trouble."

"I know. That's why Nina asked me to work with you. She wants everybody in the house to make it."

Ryan blew his whistle, calling them to attention. "Okay, people. Let's work out. Sit-ups first. Bend your legs and touch your knees with your

64

elbows. One hundred reps." He blew his whistle, signaling for them to begin.

Winston lay down on the sand, positioned his arms behind his head, and began.

"You're jerking with your back," Wendy said. "Not pulling with your stomach muscles."

"I don't *have* any stomach muscles." Winston groaned, jerking up and touching his right elbow to his left knee.

"Everybody has stomach muscles," Wendy said, bending gracefully up. "See how my abs stand out? You have to crunch your muscles."

Winston crunched as hard as he could. It felt horrible. Unnatural. Unhealthy, even. How could something good for you be called *crunching*?

Nevertheless, he sat up and crunched as if his economic future depended on it—which it did.

"Ninety-eight . . . ninety-nine . . . one hundred." Nina flopped back on the ground and took some deep breaths. Sweat rolled off her arms and legs, but she felt good. Her muscles had handled the strain with no problem. They didn't feel slack or overworked.

Ryan sat down next to her. "You look good," he said. "You kept in shape since last summer."

Nina sat up and he handed her a towel. All around them people were groaning, stretching, and cooling down. Or at least trying to. It was hard to cool down on the hot sand under the direct glare of the sun.

Several people got up and headed for the large

plastic container of water that had been set up on a table.

"Thanks for making me your assistant," she said.

"I talked to Captain Feehan about it last night. I have a lot of confidence in you. So does he. There's more paperwork involved, but you'll get fifteen percent more pay."

"Great," she said. "I can use the cash." She stared at his handsome profile. "So what have you been doing since last summer?"

Ryan didn't answer immediately, and his brown eyes moved back and forth, searching the horizon line.

That back-and-forth eye movement was something everybody developed on the job. Lifeguarding demanded a constant awareness of the ocean out there. And you never stopped scanning it for signs of trouble.

But Nina had the feeling that Ryan's eyes never left the horizon line—no matter where he was or what he was doing.

"Ryan?" she prompted.

He cleared his throat and swallowed. "I tried to go back to school. But after what happened last summer, I just couldn't focus on it. I . . ." He trailed off.

"You weren't even there. It wasn't your fault that kid drowned," Nina reminded him softly. "Why do you blame yourself?"

66

"It's complicated," he answered after a pause. "Let's not talk about it." He ran a hand through his curls and began to speak brusquely. "What did I do all year? I traveled some. Worked a little construction. Then migrated back in this direction before spring. Captain Feehan hired me again and here I am. Fourth year in a row." He stood up. "Hey, let's do some ins and outs before we break for lunch," he suggested in an impersonal tone. Clearly the exchange of confidences was over.

"You got it." Nina knew how to take a hint. She hopped to her feet, put the whistle in her mouth, and blew.

She liked Ryan. She admired Ryan. But even though they'd worked together two summers in a row, he remained something of an enigma. He'd always been hardwired. And after what had happened last summer, he'd wound himself even tighter. If he didn't loosen up—didn't lighten up—Nina was afraid he was going to break.

"Come on! Come on! Come on!"

Jessica could just barely hear the enthusiastic shouts from the beach over the splashing sound her arms and legs made as they churned through the water.

She was glad she had worn the black suit instead of the yellow. She could move better in this one. And man, she was moving fast.

Jessica had always been a good swimmer, and

the determination to excel was propelling her through the water at record speed.

Ryan had set up two flags. One in the water on a floating buoy. Another on the sand, several yards back from the shoreline.

Each person was to start from the flag on the sand, run to the water, high-step over the surf until they were waist deep, swim out to the buoy, then swim back in and run back to the flag in the sand. The run-swim-run exercise was called an in and out.

When Jessica's knee thumped against the ocean floor, she realized she was close to shore. She jumped to her feet and ran through the rest of the water, lifting her feet high and prancing over waves.

When she hit the beach, she broke into a flat-out sprint. The group erupted into cheers when she touched the flagpole.

Ryan's thumb came down on his stopwatch and he whistled. "Fastest time yet." He gave Jessica a wide smile, and her racing heart began to beat even faster. His gaze was warm, and Jessica basked in the glow of his approval.

There was something working between them. And it was giving her a boost like nothing else she'd ever experienced. She'd felt like superwoman out there.

"You even beat Ben," Winston said admiringly.

So far Ben had been the fastest. How would he react to being beaten by Jessica?

Her eyes sought him out. Oddly enough, he didn't look resentful. He looked surprised. And impressed.

For some reason it made Jessica feel good. Ben smiled at her, and the corners of her mouth lifted involuntarily. Then she caught herself. Why did she care if Ben was impressed?

The guy was a loser. A Mensa loser. She turned her attention back to Ryan and gave *him* her most winning smile.

Unfortunately Ryan wasn't looking. He was giving Elizabeth the countdown. "Three . . . two . . . one . . . *Go!*"

Elizabeth took off running toward the water. She plowed in up to her knees, then dove forward, knifing through the water toward the platform. In spite of her teasing Jessica thought Elizabeth looked sleek and strong in her simple blue one-piece with the scoop front.

As always, her form was good. But she looked slow. Really slow. . . .

Elizabeth's arms felt like lead as she stroked back to shore. Arms smacking at the surface rather than slicing through it—her form was falling apart.

Elizabeth's head had been hurting for the last half hour and her stomach was in knots. The workout had taken more out of her than she had anticipated. Now she had nothing left.

When she felt the ocean floor beneath her, she lumbered heavily to her feet and ran toward the flag. There was no shouting. No clapping. No one urging her on.

People stood around the beach in small clumps, talking among themselves. Still, she persevered, running past them and touching the pole.

She looked around for Ryan. *Where is he? Why isn't he waiting here with his stopwatch?*

Ryan stood at the edge of the station, talking with Nina. He said something to Nina, and they both turned toward Elizabeth. They exchanged a look, and Nina began walking toward her.

"Well?" Elizabeth gasped.

"He stopped timing you when your time was longer than Winston's," Nina said simply.

Elizabeth brushed her wet blond ponytail back with her hand and groaned. "I lost it out there. Just ran out of juice."

Ryan walked up to them. "Nina. Tell everybody to break and be back by three o'clock. Elizabeth, you and Winston need to come half an hour early. You both need to work on breathing." He turned away and began walking to the station, then paused and turned. "And Elizabeth?"

"Yes?"

"Be sure you eat lunch, okay?"

With that, he disappeared into the lifeguard station and shut the door.

Elizabeth's heart began a slow, dull, angry thud.

70

"I'm supposed to come back early *with Winston?*" she said in a voice of disbelief. "Nina! How can you let him talk to me like that?"

Nina shrugged helplessly. "What do you want me to do?"

"Tell him I'm not a slacker, not an airhead. I'm a good swimmer and you know it. The only reason I fell apart out there was because . . ."

Nina's eyebrows rose slightly. "Because . . . ?" she prompted.

"Because I didn't eat," Elizabeth admitted grudgingly.

Nina sighed. "Look. I know Ryan came down hard on you. But he was right. You should have eaten. You skipped a meal and it affected your swimming. He hammered you. But you won't make that mistake again, will you?"

Elizabeth frowned at Nina. "You know, Nina, you may be my best friend, but you're also Ryan's assistant. I understand you might not be able to stick up for me. But please don't patronize me."

"I'm not patronizing you," Nina protested.

"Actually you are," Elizabeth said.

Nina put her hand on Elizabeth's arm. "Let's not fight. I don't blame you for being upset. But you'll get it together after lunch."

Elizabeth felt a lump rising in her throat. Horrified, she felt a tear trickling down her cheek. She wasn't used to looking silly and inept. She missed Tom. And she felt incredibly lonely, even though her sister and her best friend were right there. "What's wrong with me?" she choked.

"Hunger," Nina said with a laugh. "You're having a weak attack and it's making you emotional. Come on. Let's go back to the house and get something to eat."

Elizabeth leaned down and pulled on her shorts, trembling with anger, embarrassment, and fatigue. She'd eat. And after lunch, she'd mop up the beach with the competition and make Ryan *and* Nina eat their words.

Chapter Seven

"I've got it!" Winston said thickly through a mouthful of bologna sandwich. "I've got the answer to my cash-flow problems."

Wendy took a bite of her tuna on an English muffin. "Oh, yeah? Let's hear it."

They were sitting on the back steps of the beach house off the kitchen, catching the afternoon breeze. Inside, everybody was making sandwiches, concocting salads, and drinking water. Through the window he could hear them laughing, talking, and teasing. Paloma Perro sat beside Wendy on the stairs and gazed hopefully at her sandwich.

"You know how in Hollywood they have tours of the stars' houses?" Winston took another bite and knitted his brows while he pulled his thoughts together.

Wendy nodded. "You bet. I've been on at least a dozen of them. It's one of my favorite things to do. I've even gotten a glimpse of some major movie stars." She broke off a piece of sandwich and held it out to Paloma. He took it delicately from her fingers, chewed vigorously, and licked his mustache, hoping to find another crumb.

"So what do you think about doing a tour of Sweet Valley Shore's celebrity beach houses? Lifestyles of the rich and fabulous at Sweet Valley Shore."

"That's brilliant. I can tell you where all the celebrities live. There are about ten along that road where Pedro Paloma's house is. It's an easy distance from the boardwalk." She took another bite of her sandwich and then gave the rest to Paloma. "Come with me," she ordered thickly.

Winston got up and followed her, sandwich in hand. Paloma trailed behind with his nose quivering.

"Let's go to my room," she instructed, her long, slender legs taking the stairs two at a time in her high-topped black sneakers worn with no socks.

Winston hurried up the two flights of stairs and entered the converted attic room. "Wow. This is nice." The room was large and spacious with a high, slanted ceiling.

Wendy opened a large suitcase and removed a drawing pad and some colored markers while Paloma circled the perimeter of the room, exploring the corners and baseboards.

"You draw?"

"Not very well. But since I was the dateless wonder last summer, I thought I'd better bring some stuff to entertain myself this year." She ripped a large sheet of paper from the pad. "We'll make a poster for your business and hang it on the boardwalk Friday afternoon. You can take your first tour on Saturday when we have the day off."

Winston happily sat down in the center of the room. He might be a washout as a lifeguard, but he felt sure that he would make a great tour guide. It would give him a chance to excel at the things he did well—gawk and make witty remarks.

Wendy handed him an orange marker and he removed the cap. "Celebrity Beachcombing," he brayed in a loud Australian accent. "Tour the exclusive, star-studded nooks and crannies of Sweet Valley Shore with the one, the only, *Winston Egbert.*"

He was imitating the Australian host of a popular show called *Fame and Fortune.* In several episodes the host conducted tours of celebrity homes and hangouts.

Wendy laughed. "I watch that show all the time."

"I think it's great that you're so up front about being into famous people. Most people try to be so cool about it. Especially if they're from Los Angeles."

"Where I grew up in Nevada, the most glamorous thing for fifty miles around was the jukebox at the diner," she said with a laugh.

Winston looked around the room. Pictures of movie stars and singers covered all of one wall. A large poster of Pedro Paloma dominated the center. He was holding a microphone, with hips thrust forward, hair flying, and heavy eyelids half closed. Definitely a heartthrob.

"First stop on the Winston Egbert Celebrity Beach House tour," he said in his Australian accent, "the home of singing sensation Pedro Paloma."

"Turn. Breathe. Turn. Breathe. Turn. Breathe."

Nina watched Elizabeth and Winston practice turning their heads, rhythmically breathing in and out in the shallow part of the water per Ryan's instructions.

She knew Elizabeth felt ridiculous doing something so remedial. And she felt bad making her do it. But she also knew Elizabeth would pull her act together this afternoon. She'd probably dust everybody and things would be cool again.

"Okay. Enough," Nina shouted.

Winston and Elizabeth both lifted their faces out of the water, and Nina grinned. "Take a break."

Winston and Elizabeth walked back up onto the shore. Winston wandered a few feet away and squatted to examine something that had washed up on the beach. Elizabeth loosened her hair, which had been pulled back into a knob at the nape of her neck. She reached for her towel and rubbed it over her hair.

"Feeling better?" Nina asked.

Elizabeth nodded. "Yeah. Listen, I'm sorry I put you on the spot earlier."

"You didn't," Nina said quickly. "I'm sorry I was so tough on you. But . . ."

"I know. You've got to do your job."

"Speaking of," Nina said. "I'd better get inside and touch base with Ryan."

Several of the other candidates were wandering up the beach, preparing for the afternoon drills.

The temperature was markedly cooler than it had been before lunch and the sky was turning a little cloudy.

Nina turned and walked up the wooden path that led to the door of the lifeguard station, hoping it wouldn't rain. She stepped inside and put her clipboard down on a table under the window. Shelves and cabinets lined every wall of the lifeguard station. There were flotation devices, lifeguard buoys, first-aid equipment, and fun stuff like volleyballs and Frisbees.

The door in the back opened and Ryan came in, munching an apple. His living quarters were attached to the back of the station and consisted of a large room with a bath and a hot plate.

The door to his room was open. The bed was neatly made, and Nina cast a surreptitious glance around. No pictures—of anybody. The bedside table held an alarm clock. Period.

"Hey!" he said in a friendly tone. "Are the troops gathering?" He grabbed a handful of papers from the desk.

"Starting to. But it's still early." She plopped

down in one of the two rockers that faced the long front windows. Ryan sat down in the other one and shuffled the papers while Nina gazed thoughtfully out at the water. "The station looks exactly the same," she said.

Ryan smiled but said nothing and continued to look through the papers.

"Here it is." He handed her a piece of paper. "I put together a preliminary schedule. Take a look and let's decide how many lifeguards we're going to need."

Nina scanned it. "You've got yourself down for every shift," she cried.

He nodded.

"You can't do that. Even *you* have to take a day off."

"I took a day off last summer," he said curtly.

"Ryan . . . ," she began.

"Tell me about SVU," he said, cutting her off.

"Tell me about you," she countered.

"I already did."

"Are you dating anybody?"

He shook his head. "No time," he said.

"You didn't date anybody last summer."

"I didn't have time," he said again.

"Ryan! You have to *make* time. If you spend all your time saving other people's lives, when are you going to live your own?"

Ryan went over to the shelf. He began pulling down the lifeguard buoys. Orange flotation devices that every lifeguard carried. Each buoy had a shoulder strap and a seven-foot nylon cord. When the lifeguards went into the water to retrieve a victim, the buoy served as a flotation device and also marked the lifeguard's position in the water in case additional help was needed.

Several of the nylon cords were tangled, and Ryan patiently began to unknot them. "Tell me about your friends. The twins."

Now we're getting somewhere. Nina smiled to herself. "Well," she began. "They're both gorgeous. They're both great. But Elizabeth is dating somebody seriously. And Jessica has had some bad experiences that have left her a little shell-shocked. But she's very available and a blast to be around. And . . ." Nina broke off, wondering whether or not to tell Ryan that Jessica was interested in him in a big way.

No, she decided. Ryan was a grown man. He'd probably get embarrassed if she made any obvious attempt at matchmaking.

The edges of Ryan's mouth turned down and he nodded, as if thinking.

"Hey! How's it going?" a strong masculine voice at the door inquired.

Nina turned. A tall, broad-shouldered male was visible only as a dark silhouette against the bright backdrop of the sunlit door. Broad shoulders formed the top of a V-shaped physique that included a narrow waist, narrow hips, and long, well-muscled legs.

The silhouette stepped inside, and Nina saw that he was an African-American guy about twenty years old, with the sexiest smile she'd seen in a long time. His skin was light brown and he wore white trunks, no shirt, and no shoes. His hair was cut short and flat across the top. Everything about him was clean-cut and squared away, but there was something in his walk, his attitude, and his smile that proclaimed him to be a free spirit. "Hi there," he said to Nina.

"Hi," she said back.

"Ryan, I need a first-aid kit."

Ryan motioned with his chin toward the shelves. "Take one of those. Nina, this is Paul Jackson. Paul, Nina Harper."

Nina smiled. "Is somebody hurt?"

"Nah. I'm running the surfboard rental stand and we're trying to get things set up."

"Then you're not a lifeguard?"

"I'm certified as a lifeguard," Paul explained, opening one of the white tins with the red heart on it and inspecting the contents. "And I worked last summer in Florida. But this year I decided I'd rather do something different. Sitting up in that chair hour after hour got old fast."

Paul unfolded a piece of paper that listed the contents of the kit, and his lips moved slightly as he checked off each item. "Band-Aids, antibiotic ointment, scissors, gauze, sterile pads. . . ." He closed the top with a snap. "All here. I'll see you guys later."

Nina watched the broad back disappear out the door. "Wow!" she said as soon as he was gone.

Ryan laughed. "I thought you said you were dating somebody."

"I am. I am," she said. "But that doesn't mean I can't look."

"Paul's a good-looking guy . . . ," Ryan agreed. There was a faint reserve in the tone, and the word *but* hung unspoken in the air.

"But what?" she asked.

Ryan frowned. "But nothing."

"Is there something about Paul you don't approve of?" she asked.

Ryan reached for his T-shirt, pulled it on over his head, and slid his feet into thongs. "I'm not sure how serious Paul is. About his job—or anything else."

Chapter Eight

The metal whistle made a sharp, authoritative sound, and Elizabeth fought a little stab of irritation. Every time Ryan blew that whistle, it sounded like a personal rebuke.

"Okay, people!" he shouted. "Shoulder the buoy and start getting used to it. Where you go, it goes. It never leaves your side. Repeat. It *never* leaves your side."

Elizabeth shifted her shoulder, letting the long buoy rest more comfortably behind her. It wasn't heavy, but it would take some getting used to. When lifeguarding in the pool, she had been taught to use her hands for victim retrieval. But as Ryan and Nina had both explained and demonstrated, in the ocean you didn't want to be in physical contact with the victim if at all possible. Fighting waves, a riptide, and a panicky swimmer all at the same time was impossible. With a buoy the lifeguard could tow the victim in, have both arms to swim with, and avoid being dragged under by the victim.

"Now we're going to jog. Three miles. No shoes." He pointed up the beach. "Anybody think they'll have trouble?" His questioning eyes met Elizabeth's.

Elizabeth refused to blink. Did he really think she was going to demur at three miles? That was a stroll in the park.

When nobody said anything, he smiled. "Actually we're going to be jogging in the water."

Everybody began to laugh. Running thigh deep in the water was a different story altogether. Even Elizabeth smiled.

"Try to keep up," he said. "Everybody follow me."

Ryan took off toward the water. When thirty sets of feet hit the water, the foam splashed in every direction. There was a lot of cutting up and clowning going on behind Ryan.

Elizabeth wondered if he would turn and tell them to settle down. He did turn. But he didn't chew anybody out. He smiled and seemed happy that they were having fun.

They ran parallel with the empty beach. The gathering clouds and chilly air had driven all the sunbathers indoors.

Within minutes Elizabeth felt her thigh muscles working hard against the resistance of the water.

A tall, redheaded lanky guy ran beside her.

"Can you talk and run at the same time?" he asked.

"I think so," she said, her voice sounding a bit breathless.

"I'm Kerry Janowitz," he said.

"Elizabeth Wakefield."

"Have you ever lifeguarded before?"

"Never on a beach," she admitted. "Only at the pool. When I was in high school. What about you?"

"Same thing."

"Where do you go to school now?"

"I'm actually between colleges at the moment. I went to Stanford last year, but I want to be where it's cold. So I'm trying to transfer to Colorado. Haven't heard anything yet, though."

"You're a skier?"

"I love skiing," he confirmed. "If I don't get into school next fall, I might try to get a job at a ski resort."

"Lifeguarding in the summer. Ski resorts in the winter. Not a bad life." She laughed.

"Don't get the wrong idea," he said. "I'm a good student. I'm just bad with deadlines. I sent in my transfer request a month late."

Elizabeth tried to nod. "Where are you living?"

Kerry pointed to a large house set back from the beach. "There. I'm rooming with a bunch of guys from Stanford and Paula McFee." He pointed to a petite young woman with long, straight black hair. "That's Paula. She's a soph-

84

omore at UVA. Tell me who you know."

Very quickly Elizabeth pointed out her house-mates and told Kerry their names and vital statistics.

"You know," she said, "I'm not nearly as klutzy and dizzy as everybody thinks."

Kerry laughed. "I don't think you're klutzy or dizzy."

Elizabeth felt better. So far, she was doing great. Her muscles were working hard, but she was handling it fine. Ahead several people were beginning to look winded and were slowing down.

At the head of the pack Ryan plowed forward as if he were running on a clay track wearing cushion-soled shoes. His powerful legs plunged effortlessly through the water. Jessica pulled ahead and ran beside him.

Elizabeth lifted her own legs higher, determined to work at least as hard as her sister, when suddenly . . . "Ouch!" she cried. A sharp pain on the bottom of her foot caused her to stumble. Falling, she reached out for Kerry's hand to steady herself.

Her cry brought the group to a halt. Ryan turned, and the group parted so he could wade quickly between them to see what had happened.

Before Elizabeth had time to protest, Ryan had lifted her out of the water as if she weighed nothing.

Ryan carried her up to the shore and set her

gently down on the sand. He knelt and examined her foot, which was covered with blood now.

Ryan pulled off his T-shirt and used it to wipe away the blood. "You stepped on something sharp," he said. "Probably a shell." His large hands were gentle as he turned her foot slightly. "Does that hurt?"

She shook her head.

He manipulated the foot forward and backward. "That?"

"No."

He sat back on his heels. "Good. You didn't sprain your ankle or anything. And that cut's not deep enough for stitches. Salt water's a good antiseptic, but I don't think you should run on it anymore today."

Elizabeth's shoulders slumped. "But I—"

"No arguments. Wait here, and we'll pick you up on the way back. I'll help you to the station and then drive you to your house in the dune buggy."

He looked up and down the beach. There was no one in sight. "Kerry, why don't you stay with Elizabeth so she doesn't have to sit here by herself?"

It took all of Elizabeth's self-control not to reach out and punch him. "Kerry doesn't need to stay with me," she snapped.

"I don't like women to be on the beach by themselves."

"I'm not a child." Elizabeth glowered at him.

86

Ryan looked surprised at her reaction. "I'm not trying to treat you like a kid. I guess I should have said nobody—male or female—should be on a deserted beach by themselves. It's not safe."

"I don't need anybody to baby-sit me," Elizabeth insisted. "I'm fine. I'll just sit here and wait for you guys to get back."

He looked uncertain, and she felt her eyes flash dangerously. Ryan seemed to sense that she was spoiling for a fight, and he capitulated. "Okay. Here. Take this." He removed the whistle from around his neck and held it out. "If for any reason you get nervous, blow. We'll hear it and come back."

Elizabeth tried to take the whistle politely, but she was so irritated, she snatched it instead. By doing so, she knew she appeared childish and petulant.

"We won't be long," he assured her.

With that he took off running, and the group fell in behind him. Nina cast a sympathetic look over her shoulder and waved good-bye. But Jessica fell in beside Ryan without a backward look.

Elizabeth fluttered her fingers and groaned slightly. She was jinxed. Absolutely jinxed. This whole lifeguard thing was going from bad to worse.

It was as if she had stepped into some parallel universe where Jessica could do no wrong and Elizabeth could do no right.

Ryan Taylor hated her. He thought she was an incompetent klutz. He thought she was a child. She was never going to make it onto the squad.

Maybe that was a good thing. Having to spend the whole summer taking orders from somebody like him would keep her blood pressure in a constant state of elevation. Who wanted to spend their whole summer being treated like an imbecile by a man with a body like Hercules and a personality like Patton?

She had to admit, though, his hands had been incredibly gentle. And when he'd looked at her with those brown eyes . . .

Elizabeth stood up, feeling suddenly agitated, guilty, and embarrassed. What was the matter with her? She had a boyfriend. His name was Tom. And her sister, who was absolutely available, had her eye on Ryan. Even thinking about Ryan in that way was wrong. And stupid, silly, and humiliating.

A swim. That's what she needed. A brisk swim would clear her head and pass the time. And Ryan had said himself that salt water was a good antiseptic. The water would be good for her foot.

She eased the buoy off her shoulder and put it down on the sand next to the whistle. The waves were curling higher than they had this morning and were breaking hard close in.

She stroked out into the sea, diving under the waves, enjoying the unregimented swim and the push and tug of the cold water.

*   *   *

Poor Elizabeth, Nina thought as she jogged along beside Ben. She knew how much of Elizabeth's ego was tied up in excelling and being trusted.

Her best friend's pride was taking a major beating. No doubt about it, there was some very weird karma in the air.

Maybe Elizabeth and Jessica were on some kind of wheel. If one was up, the other automatically had to be down.

Elizabeth's luck was in the Dumpster, but Jessica was doing great.

Ahead of her and Ben, Jessica jogged easily beside Ryan. Jess smiled and flirted and laughed, and Nina could hear the sound of Ryan's laughter floating back toward her.

Good for Jessica, Nina thought. Maybe she was exactly what Ryan needed. She was fun. She was flirty. She was aggressive. And she didn't take no for an answer. It wouldn't hurt Ryan to have a little summer fun. Maybe he'd change his mind about being on duty every single day.

"How much farther?" Ben asked.

"We'll turn around at that pier," she answered, pointing to the wooden pier on which the Sand Bar was situated.

Nina didn't know much about Ben yet, except that he was an old friend of Bryan's from high school and he seemed to enjoy teasing Jessica.

Nina remembered enough grade school psychology to know what that meant. He obviously liked Jessica but didn't know how to get her attention without making her angry.

"I think I got off on the wrong foot with your friend," he said, trying to sound casual.

Nina smiled. "I know you did." Her arms pumped at her sides and her legs slushed through the thin white foam that floated on the surface of the water.

"Any tips on how to get on her good side?"

Nina bit her lip, thinking hard. Ben seemed like a nice guy. And according to Bryan, he was brilliant and had always been quite a ladies' man.

So why was he striking out with Jessica?

Probably because Ben wasn't her type, and Jessica wasn't his. "Maybe you should step back and look around a little more," she answered evasively.

"You mean you don't think I have a chance?"

Nina wasn't a meddler by nature. But if Ryan and Jessica were going to get it together—and it looked as if they might—she didn't want Ben to mess things up.

"I think there are lots of girls on the beach and most of them would think you were an incredible catch. Like Rachel from South Beach."

It was a shot in the dark, but she could tell by the little catch of his breath that she'd hit the mark.

"There's nothing between me and Rachel," Ben said.

"But there used to be?"

Ben came to halt and put his hands on his hips as if he were resting. Nina stopped beside him, and they let the rest of the pack pass them by. When they were out of earshot, Nina gave him an encouraging smile. "Well? Want to tell me about it?"

Ben rubbed his hand through his short, clipped black hair and adjusted the buoy on his shoulder. "I guess I should explain. Rachel and I dated at University of Chicago. She talked me into coming down here to work this summer. But then we had a fight around exam time and I broke up with her. It looked like the summer job and house thing was down the tube. I was bummed about that because I really wanted to spend the summer at the beach. So when Bryan called and said he was looking for somebody to take his place, I jumped on it." He gave her a sly grin. "Didn't want to miss a chance to meet some bathing beauties."

"Something tells me Rachel's not too happy about the breakup . . . ," Nina said.

"What makes you think that?"

"The fact that she tried to take Jessica's head off with a Frisbee at orientation. I saw the throw, and it looked deliberate to me."

Ben laughed. "Wow. Not too much gets by you, does it?"

"Lifeguarding trains you to keep your eyes open," she said.

"Well, Nina Harper. Bryan was right. You're smart. You're straightforward. And you're practical. So tell me straight. Do I have a chance with Jessica?"

"You're not her type," Nina said, trying to sound kind.

"And Ryan is?"

"I hope so," Nina said, beginning to jog again. "I really hope so. He deserves some happiness. And so does she."

"I have to stop," Winston gasped.

"No, you don't," Wendy said.

"Yes, I do. I'm going to faint," he huffed.

"No, you're not," Wendy insisted.

"My legs are about to fall off."

Wendy laughed. "Don't think about it. Run through the pain. Make a friend of pain."

"Pain and I don't have a comfortable relationship."

"Then just ignore it and think about your business. I think ten dollars a head is a good price." She gasped. "Look out there."

Winston looked in the direction of her pointing finger and saw Pedro Paloma walking a basset hound along the pier. He wore floppy white cotton trousers and an open chambray shirt. His unbraided hair flew out behind him in the wind.

"Isn't he gorgeous?"

"Why don't you go up there and say hello?"

Winston suggested, veering toward the sand so he could run in shallower water.

Wendy followed. "What? Just go over and talk to him? And come back here?"

Winston paused and clutched his chest like he was in terrible pain. "Sure," he panted. "Now's the perfect time. Go tell him how much you enjoy his music. And ask him if he knows CPR. I think I'm having a heart attack."

"Not for a million dollars," Wendy said firmly, ignoring his dire health prediction.

"Why not?"

"Because I'd just look like some starstruck fan."

"You *are* a starstruck fan. Why wouldn't he want to meet you? He probably loves meeting fans."

"Not fans who look like me," she said firmly.

Winston felt truly at a loss. He didn't know much about women. But they all seemed to have some insecurity gene that men didn't.

Winston knew he was no hunk. But it didn't occur to him that he *needed* to be a hunk in order to be attractive to women.

Sure, girls went gaga over big muscles and square jaws. But they also responded to warmth, wit, kindness, and intelligence. Winston had those qualities in abundance.

So did Wendy. She was a great person. So why was she so sure no guy would be interested in her?

"Besides, we don't have anything in common," she added, pulling the bottom of her plain black tank suit down and giving each leg a loud elastic snap. Her straight hair hung in wet strands over her shoulders, but her gray eyes shone like diamonds.

Pedro and the dog stood at the end of the pier now. The dog's ears blew backward in the wind like Pedro's hair.

Winston took some deep breaths. His heart rate seemed to be returning to normal. "Yes, you do. He's got a dog. You've got a dog. *Voilà*. There you go. Something to talk about. The perfect conversational gambit."

"I can't do that," Wendy said quietly.

"Yes, you can."

"Let's not talk about it anymore, okay?" she pleaded.

"Okay, sure," Winston said.

The group had turned and was splashing back in their direction. "Slackers!" the group all shouted and teased.

"Let's finish up on the beach," Ryan shouted. "There's too much current now. Notice how quickly it changed."

The group cheered and followed Ryan up onto the sand.

"Come on," Wendy urged. "It'll be easy running on the sand after running in the water."

Winston dug his long toes down into the sand and anchored himself. "No. I can't run anymore. On land *or* sea."

Wendy pushed him until he was forced to release his toehold. "If you stop thinking about what you can't do, it's amazing what you *can* do."

Winston watched her slender arms pump and her long, graceful legs move as she hurried to catch up with the pack. She waved her arm at him to follow. *Look who's talking,* he thought. Wendy had everything in the world going for her—except confidence. All she needed was a little boost to the old self-esteem.

He looked back over his shoulder at Pedro Paloma. He was sitting down on his haunches and touching his nose to his dog's. The dog wagged his tail and wiggled with enthusiasm.

Pedro Paloma was a good-looking guy, all right. And he probably could have his pick of any woman on the beach.

So why was he at a beautiful beach on a perfect day all by himself, kissing his dog and not a woman?

Elizabeth felt the gathering swell of a huge wave lifting her higher as she treaded water out beyond the surf. In front of her she could see the beach. The current ran parallel with the beach, moving her steadily southward. *A lateral current,* Ryan had called it this morning when he'd lectured them on hazards and topography.

She kicked her legs, preparing to swim in before she got too far down the beach. She didn't want to have to walk a long way back to her buoy and whistle on her cut foot.

Suddenly and without warning the current shifted, flowing hard from the shore in the direction of the ocean.

Elizabeth tried to swim against it. She kicked and stroked, but she couldn't make any headway. It was as if the ocean had her by the ankle and was pulling her in the opposite direction.

Oh, no! I'm caught in a riptide! She gasped and accidentally sucked in a mouthful of water. *Don't panic!* she warned herself as she coughed and sputtered. *If you panic, you'll die!* But it was too late. She was already panicking, trying to scream, breathe, and swim—all at the same time.

As they approached the Sweet Valley Shore, Jessica was winded and her legs felt heavy.

"Don't think you have to keep up with me," Ryan said kindly. "This is just a practice run."

"I like keeping up with you," Jessica responded, working hard to sound as if she wasn't tired. She cut her eyes sideways and caught him looking at her legs.

Ryan had to be impressed with her stamina. There was no way Jessica was going to look like a weakling now. So far she'd kept pace with him the whole time and kept up a stream of light chatter. He'd laughed several times and complimented her on her strength and enthusiasm.

She hoped Ben was close enough behind them

to overhear their conversation. What a creep! Jessica had attracted more than her share of creeps in the past. Men who were nasty. Mean. More interested in tearing her down than building her up. Men like Mike McAllery, her ex-husband, the arrested adolescent she had impulsively married early in her freshman year. The marriage had been brief, but stormy and hurtful.

After Mike there had been James Montgomery—the man who'd tried to rape her. She shivered at the memory. Sometimes she still had nightmares about that.

She sensed tension in Ryan beside her. Then he came to a sudden stop.

Jessica's eyes flickered over the beach to see what he was looking at. That was when she saw the buoy and whistle alone on the sand.

"Where is Elizabeth?" she heard Nina murmur along with several other people.

The significance of the abandoned gear was just beginning to register when she felt the sand beneath her shake. Ryan had pushed off the wet surface and was streaking toward the water, pulling his goggles into place.

Jessica's head snapped toward the ocean and she screamed. A hundred yards out her sister flailed frantically.

Jessica began to run, determined to swim out with Ryan. But a strong hand caught her arm. "Let me go!" she shouted.

"Wait here," Ben said, tightening his grip.

"My sister's out there," Jessica wailed.

Ben put an arm around her shoulders. "I know. But let Ryan handle this. He's the professional."

It was like being in a blender. Currents swirled in every direction, pushing her, pulling her, and occasionally dragging Elizabeth under. Water and pressure roared in her ears like an engine.

Elizabeth scissored her legs. Desperately. Clumsily. Her arms windmilled, sometimes meeting the resistance of the water and sometimes beating the air as the ocean tossed her about. She was exhausted and disoriented. Unsure now in which direction the shore lay.

Over the sound of the wind and the surf, she heard a shout.

Through a veil of salty water she saw something red. Seconds later Ryan emerged out of the foam like Poseidon. "Grab this," he instructed, throwing his red buoy toward her. It landed inches away. With one last surge of effort Elizabeth propelled herself toward the flotation device and clutched it against her chest, wrapping her arms tightly around it.

"Hold on!" he shouted.

Choking and sobbing with relief, Elizabeth let her legs float out behind her as Ryan towed her back toward the beach. He plowed through the surf, both muscular arms stroking in steady rhythm.

He never wavered as the waves pummeled his body and crashed around them.

His strength was incredible, and in a matter of minutes they were safely back in hip-deep water. He slid his arm out of the harness as Jessica, Nina, and Winston came running out.

Elizabeth tried to stand, but her legs collapsed. Ryan caught her before she could fall, picking her up and carrying her toward the beach as if she were a child. A sudden feeling of exhaustion washed over her, and she let her head fall against his muscular chest. She could hear his heart pounding. Pounding almost as hard as her own.

He placed her on the sand and gently removed his arms. Jessica knelt and rubbed her hands up and down Elizabeth's trembling arms. Ryan stood and walked in a circle, breathing deeply and trying to compose himself.

Elizabeth watched him, waiting for him to say something comforting. Something kind. She had never been so terrified in her life.

Instead his tanned face darkened and his eyes narrowed. "I can't believe you went out there for a swim," he said in a steely tone. "Alone."

Elizabeth's eyes opened slightly wider. *Uh-oh!*

"You went out there with no buddy . . . no lifeguard . . . no buoy." His tongue touched his upper lip and he hesitated, obviously trying to control his temper. "Do you have any idea how stupid that was? What is the most basic and fundamental rule of water safety?" he asked.

Nina stepped forward and put a restraining hand on Ryan's arm. "Ryan!" she began. "Don't—"

Ryan shook off her hand. Elizabeth saw the rest of the group back up a little, embarrassed and afraid.

"I'm sorry," Elizabeth began in a small voice.

"Tell me and tell everybody so nobody makes that kind of mistake," he insisted.

"Never go in the water alone," Elizabeth said. Her voice sounded high and thin. The wind whipped her wet hair around her face and she raked it away with trembling fingers.

"I ought to disqualify you right here and now."

Every single person drew in their breath. Except for the sound of the surf and the cry of a gull, there was a tense, heavy silence. Elizabeth waited miserably for Ryan to tell her to leave the beach and not come back.

But he said nothing. They stared at each other. His throat quivered, and she watched the muscle in his jaw work.

After a few agonizing moments he tore his eyes away from Elizabeth's face and shook his head, as if clearing it. "That's it for today," Ryan said. He began walking down the beach toward the life-guard station. "Nina. You or somebody else can drive back and get Elizabeth in the dune buggy."

He was so angry, nobody ventured to accompany him. The group gave him a long head start before they began filing back down the beach toward the station.

"Wait here," Nina said softly. "I'll be back."

Elizabeth stared after the disappearing group with her lip trembling. Jessica put a hand on her arm. "If I wasn't so relieved you're okay, I'd be really angry with you, too."

"I'm sorry I scared you."

Jessica grinned. "I'm not angry because of that," she said with a laugh. "I was really getting somewhere with Ryan, and it all went up in smoke when he had to go and rescue you." She reached back and lifted her long blond hair off her shoulders and stretched her neck. "Not to worry. He wants me. I know he does. I'm getting all the signals."

Elizabeth's lips were trembling, but she managed to stretch them in a smile. "That's . . . great, Jess. Really great," she squeaked, feeling as if the sun had just permanently disappeared behind the clouds.

Chapter
Nine

"If you get lost, look for the red propeller beanie," Winston shouted. He projected his voice over the salty wind that ruffled the shorts and shirts of the twenty or so sightseers who'd assembled on the boardwalk for Winston Egbert's Celebrity Beach House Tour. Not a bad turnout, considering the beach wasn't really open yet.

He'd found the propeller beanie this morning in one of the many gift and novelty shops along the boardwalk. In a place called the Treasure Chest.

"Okay, let's get going. And everybody keep their eyes peeled. You never know when you're going to spot a celebrity."

Twenty minutes later Winston led the group toward Dune Boulevard after taking them through an alley behind an apartment complex owned by megastar Paula Cunard's mother. He'd shown them the hole (and let them take turns peeping

102

through it) in the high hedge that shielded the home of Walter Collier, the notoriously reclusive performance artist. And they'd examined the litter barrel behind Corny's, a private club that catered to the local glitterati.

He walked with a spring in his step, feeling more optimistic about his prospects for the summer. It had been three days since they'd started training. Three days of pure, unadulterated hell as far as Winston was concerned.

Deep down, he knew he wasn't cut out for the life of a daring lifeguard. But an intrepid tour guide? That he could do.

His pocket bulged with ten-dollar bills collected from his tour group. If business remained this brisk, he'd be in the money in no time at all. "To the left, you can see the beautiful summer home of Renee Montclair, the star of *I Believe in Miracles*." He gestured with his long, bony arm to the right. "And on the right, the modest weekend getaway bungalow belonging to Dan Jamison and Melody Geffin."

"I thought they were divorced," an older lady commented, peering at the house over the tops of her sunglasses.

"They were. Then they got married again," a heavyset teenage girl answered. "According to *L.A. Entertainment Gossip,* the marriage isn't working out too well."

"Isn't that a shame," the older lady clucked.

"Look! I think I see somebody," a young man shouted.

The crowd surged through the gate onto the property.

"Is it Dan Jamison?" the teenage girl asked. "If it's him, I'll die. I'll just die."

"Folks," Winston protested. "I think we should stay on the road."

"Ask him if he's happy with Melody," joked a boy in baggy tropical shorts, high-top red sneakers, and a white mesh T-shirt. "If he's not, I sure could be."

His young girlfriend gave him a sour smile through her braces. "Ha, ha!"

The front door opened, and a huge man came hurrying up the walk. White slacks. White deck shoes. And a white shirt. *Moby Dick*, Winston thought.

His very presence and size herded them backward. The group scurried off the walk and back onto the road, taking refuge behind Winston.

"This is private property," the man said gruffly. He pulled the gate shut and locked it with a pointed clang.

"Is that a bodyguard?" a middle-aged woman in a pink shift and sun hat asked as he walked huffily back into the house.

"Oh, yes," Winston said, trying to sound like he had the inside scoop. *Unless he's the cook*, he mentally amended.

"I thought bodyguards were supposed to be handsome. That man wasn't handsome at all," the woman complained.

Winston smiled brightly, determined not to let this minor setback spoil the convivial mood of the tour group. "Speaking of handsome men . . . please follow me."

A few yards down they found themselves outside the open gates of a modest two-story house with a porch on the side. "This unassuming edifice," Winston intoned in his best tour guide voice, "is the summer residence of singer Pedro Paloma. If some of you are wondering who Pedro Paloma is—"

"I know who he is," a teenage girl with a red ponytail said quickly. "He's the one who sings 'The Night.' And he's beautiful."

"He's gorgeous," her blond friend concurred. "I mean like drop-dead super-deluxe gorgeous."

"I saw him sing in Los Angeles last summer," another teenage girl said.

A high-pitched, earsplitting squeal practically lifted Winston out of his sneakers. "There he is!" the redhead screamed.

The front door had opened and Pedro Paloma stood there, frozen like a deer. He wore pajama bottoms and no shirt, and he had obviously just retrieved the newspaper from his front porch.

The redheaded girl lurched forward, but her friend grabbed her by the back of her T-shirt and yanked. "Be cool," she admonished.

"But it's Pedro Paloma! I have to get his autograph."

The front door shut with a bang, and immediately the blinds over the front windows closed.

A collective sigh of disappointment waffled through the crowd.

"Now, folks, don't be disappointed. Touring the homes of the stars is like bird watching. A celebrity sighting is an event for the diary . . . even if it is only a fleeting glimpse. Let's keep moving."

Whistling jauntily, he led the group a little farther down Dune Boulevard.

"Wow!" A man in Bermuda shorts whistled, pointing through the open gates of a lavishly landscaped estate. "Who lives here?"

"The one, the only, Chi Chi Guzbar."

"The movie star who does the commercials for Miracle Flower Food?"

"That's the one," Winston said happily.

"I want a flower as a memento," a woman said. She stepped inside the yard and into one of the flower beds and broke off a pink stem.

"Me too," said an older lady with white hair and a big shopping bag. She picked off a lavender-colored flower and a bright red geranium. "I want one for each of my grandchildren."

The next thing Winston knew, twenty tourists were tramping through Chi Chi Guzbar's flower bed, destroying it. Winston looked nervously around. Somebody had gone to a lot of trouble to plant those flowers. He wouldn't blame them if they sent out a bodyguard or two to shoo his group away.

No burly caretaker appeared, but Winston did find himself staring eye to eye with the lens of a security camera mounted beside the gate.

There was a low buzz as the camera scanned the group.

"Uhhh, I think we'd better move on," Winston said. Somewhere there was a monitor connected to that camera. And somewhere, somebody was watching them. But the group paid no attention.

Behind the house Winston heard a disturbing sound. Barking. "Ahhh, folks," he said.

His flock continued plucking blooms from the flower beds.

The barking grew louder.

"Folks," he repeated nervously. "I think we'd better cool it."

"Oh," the lady in the straw hat cooed. "Look at the—"

"Run!" Winston screamed as two sleek brown Doberman pinschers came careening around the corner of the house, snarling and barking. "They *released the dogs!"*

The guy in the white mesh T-shirt let out a yell and grabbed his girlfriend's hand. Flowers scattered in every direction as she threw her bouquet in the air and headed for the road.

The middle-aged lady in the shift ran in one direction and the redheaded teenage girl and her blond friend ran in the opposite direction.

Winston heard the crunching of tires on the road. He looked over his shoulder and saw a bus. "Stop!" he shouted, running out into the pavement and spreading his arms. "Stop!"

Squealing air brakes brought the bus to a skidding halt.

"Get in the bus!" Winston yelled.

The door opened with a whoosh, and the twenty tourists stampeded toward the door. Winston ran around to board the bus himself, but the entrance was so crowded, he couldn't get to the first step.

Behind him the snarling and barking had reached a frenzied and hysterical pitch.

"Let me on. Let me on!" he begged, trying hard to clutch the rail by the door and pull himself aboard. But there was so much chattering and exclaiming, no one heard.

He fell back onto the road just as the door closed with another whoosh. There was a screech and a roar, and the bus moved on.

Winston rolled to the side of the road, expecting the two dogs to pounce on him. He could hear them barking hysterically a few yards away.

A few seconds passed, and when nothing happened, Winston slowly opened his eyes.

Amazingly enough, the dogs remained inside the perimeter of the gate. They barked. They snarled. And they paced back and forth along the drive. But they didn't try to leave the yard.

Electronic collars! Winston realized with a rush of relief. The dogs wore electronic collars that delivered a shock if they crossed a wire that ran underground. He'd seen a television show about that. The dogs wouldn't set a paw beyond the entranceway.

Giggling with relief, Winston stood. His propeller beanie sat in the road and he retrieved it, blowing off the dust. He placed the beanie on his head and gave the propeller a cocky spin. "So there," he said, thumbing his nose at the camera.

That set the dogs off again. But Winston paid no attention. He headed back in the direction of the boardwalk, feeling that his first tour had been a success in spite of the attack dogs.

It was a great day. He had a pocket full of cash. The sun was high in the sky. And there was enough breeze to keep the propeller on his beanie spinning. "The night," he began to sing, arranging his face in the heavy-lidded romantic expression that Pedro Paloma wore in the poster in Wendy's room. "Is beautiful . . ."

He lifted his voice and delivered the next line in a shimmering, throbbing falsetto. "You . . . are beautiful. . . ." His voice grew louder and more dramatic as he sang Pedro Paloma's best-known ballad. He drew out the last note in a high, thin voice. When his wind petered out, he heard someone chuckle.

Winston broke off and whirled around. The man who had been pointed out to him as Captain Feehan sat in the cab of the GMC truck he drove, watching him through the open window with a great deal of amusement. "Mr. Egbert?" he ventured.

Blushing to the roots of his hair, Winston walked over to the truck. He'd been singing so loudly, he hadn't heard it approach. "Yes, sir?"

"I'm Captain Feehan." Captain Feehan extended his hand, and Winston shook it tentatively, feeling incredibly foolish. "I'd like to have a little talk with you about your tour business."

Winston hadn't had much interaction with law enforcement in his time, but he couldn't help but feel that Captain Feehan's interest was not a good sign. "Is there a problem?"

"Several people have called in with complaints," Captain Feehan began.

"Complaints? About what?"

"Trespassing. Damaging private property. Peeping." He handed Winston a rolled-up piece of paper. It was Winston's poster. Obviously Captain Feehan had removed it from the boardwalk.

"Unfortunately I'm going to have to ask you to terminate Winston Egbert's Celebrity Beach House Tour."

"Am I in trouble?"

Captain Feehan smiled. "Not unless you ignore this friendly warning. The folks who live on this beach are entitled to the same degree of privacy

110

that you and your friends have. Would you like it if a group of tourists showed up at your house, picked your flowers, walked all over your yard, and peered in your windows?"

"I guess not," Winston admitted.

"I'm sorry to put you out of business, but I just can't allow it to continue."

"Yes, sir, I understand. No more tours."

Captain Feehan smiled. "Aren't you trying out for the lifeguard squad?"

"Yes."

Captain Feehan pushed his hat back on his head and grinned. "Don't worry. Once you're on the squad, Ryan will keep you too busy to lead any more tours."

Chapter Ten

Jessica stood on the landing outside her bedroom and adjusted the skirt of her dress. The door to Wendy's room was open just a crack, and she could hear Wendy giving a dejected Winston a pep talk.

"You will to get on the squad," Wendy's voice insisted. "You've just got to think positive and try a little harder."

Jessica shook her head. She had serious doubts about that. Winston wasn't doing too well. He was slow. And he was clumsy. Jessica, however, had continued to excel. She smiled and felt a shiver of anticipation. Ryan had complimented her several times. Jessica hoped tonight would be the night for her and Ryan to finally get together. There was a dance tonight at the Sand Bar. No band. But Nina had assured her that everybody in the area showed up for the dances. Jessica hoped "everybody" included Ryan.

She walked carefully down the stairs. Her green silk dress fit tightly over the bodice and waist. The flared skirt was short, and she wore green sandals that matched.

A low whistle greeted her arrival at the bottom of the stairs in the living room. Ben sat back in the blue leather recliner, watching her with frank admiration over the top of a newspaper. "Wow!"

Jessica felt her cheeks redden slightly when his blue eyes gave her a long, head-to-toe look. She felt gratified and embarrassed at the same time.

"Are we going to the same dance?" he asked in an amused voice. "If we are, I'm seriously underdressed." He popped the footrest down and sat up, gesturing toward his jeans and sneakers.

Jessica's gratification turned to irritation. Ben's "amused" voice always sounded smug and superior to her. "Are you trying to tell me I'm overdone?" she snapped, suddenly self-conscious. She knew she was probably more dressed up than anybody else, but she wanted to stand out. Now she was afraid she looked ridiculous, and she was embarrassed.

"I don't think I said anything like that," Ben said with a defensive laugh. "Why does everything I say make you mad?"

"Because everything you say sounds like a put-down," she explained.

His blue eyes turned sad in a parody of misunderstood hurt, and he stood up and put his hand to his chest. "Would I put you down?"

"Considering the fact that you've done nothing but put me down since we met, my answer would have to be yes." And with that Jessica turned and shouted up the stairs. "Nina! Are you coming?"

"You'd better get going," Elizabeth said.

"Nina!" Jessica called again. "It's time to go."

"I'm coming," Nina shouted over her shoulder. She stood at the foot of Elizabeth's bed with her thumbs hitched in the pockets of her white jeans. Her flat midriff peeked out from under the white sleeveless cotton shirt she'd tied under her bust.

"You look great," Elizabeth added with a smile. "I hope you have a good time."

"I'd feel a lot better if you were there," Nina said, removing a lipstick from her pocket and dabbing it on her lower lip. "It's the first dance of the summer. The last one before the beaches open and everything cranks into high gear."

"I really don't want to go," Elizabeth said. "I've left two messages on Tom's voice mail and . . ."

"He still hasn't called you back?"

Elizabeth shook her head. "He's probably been just as busy as I have getting settled in. But tonight's Saturday, so I ought to be able to reach him."

"If you reach him, will you come to the dance afterward?"

"I'll think about it," Elizabeth promised.

"Look, Elizabeth," Nina said with an edge in her voice. "I know you're still freaked out about what happened the other day. And I know you think Ryan hates you. But he doesn't. And you've done well the last two days. So get over it, would you?"

Elizabeth smiled tightly and tried not to feel angry. She'd busted her butt the last two days, determined to do some damage control on her image. Ryan had chewed her out once or twice for goofing up. But he'd chewed everybody out when they'd goofed up. Still, Elizabeth couldn't help feeling she was being singled out for criticism.

"I am over it," she insisted. "But I'm tired. I don't feel like dancing. And I want some time to myself. Okay?"

"Okay," Nina said. She hesitated. "Are we okay? I mean, you and me?"

"Have a good time," Elizabeth said with a smile, hoping Nina didn't notice that she avoided answering the question.

Nina paused, then returned the smile. "Okay. Come on over if you change your mind."

When she left, Elizabeth turned over and groaned, wishing everybody would get out of the house so she could be alone.

Wendy twirled under Winston's arm and spun around him like a top. Several people on the dance

115

floor whistled their approval, and Wendy smiled happily.

The band pounded out a funky late-sixties garage band rock song, and Wendy thought how nice it was to have somebody to dance with. Last summer she'd sat out a whole lot more songs than she'd danced to.

It wasn't that she was unattractive—it was just that compared to all the incredible beauties that had assembled at the Sand Bar for the dances, she'd faded into the wall.

And whenever that had happened, she went from a reasonably well-adjusted, intelligent college junior to a wobbling, weak mass of insecurity who felt as if she had to apologize for her very existence.

She eyed the crowd. There were a bunch of hunky guys. And some of them were looking at her. Now that she was getting a chance to show her stuff a little, maybe she didn't come off like such a wallflower.

On the other hand, she reflected wryly, it was possible they were looking at Winston. It wasn't every day you saw a tall guy with long legs and long arms wearing bright, baggy tropical shorts, a matching shirt, and a red propeller beanie.

The music came to a stop, and the crowd applauded.

"What do you want to drink?" Winston asked.

"Any kind of soda," she replied.

"Grab a table and I'll be back in a flash."

Wendy lifted her brown hair up off her neck and fanned her face with her hand as she walked through the large, barnlike place. The Sand Bar had a long bar, a dance floor, lots of tables, and a stage where several nights a week they featured live entertainment—like Pedro Paloma.

It was exactly the kind of dance hall you would expect to find on a beach packed with college students. The decor was minimal. Maybe even non-existent. The walls and floors were constructed from shingled gray planks. Here and there a fishing net hung from the ceiling—but that was the only concession to decorating. That and the string of Christmas lights that hung behind the bar.

Nightspots like the Sand Bar didn't need a lot of decorating. The patrons were colorful enough. Like many of the beach bars and restaurants, it was built over the water and surrounded on three sides with a deck. If it got too hot inside, people could step out for fresh air and conversation.

Tonight, though, the air was cool. Not many people seemed eager to stand outside. It was still early in the summer.

Too early for the kind of crowds that usually packed the Sand Bar. Tonight it was mostly beach employees, aspiring lifeguards, and locals.

Wendy saw several familiar faces. People who worked in the shops and restaurants. And people who were trying out for the other squads.

The crowd parted, and Rachel came walking through with the entire South Beach crew. As usual Kyle Fisher wore his fishing hat and walked beside Rachel. Behind them came Tina Fong, a petite Korean American. Danielle Dodge, big and blond. Hunter Pickering—a tall, good-looking redhead. Jack Fromton, a nondescript type with brown hair that would turn bright blond by the end of the summer. And Kristi Bjorn, the pale Norwegian girl. Prematurely balding Mickey Esposito walked with the two new people—a tall African American girl and a blond guy with a ponytail.

They came to a stop at a table a few feet from Wendy and waited while Kyle and a couple of the other guys scouted enough chairs for everybody.

Wendy took a deep breath and stood. It was time to act like a grown-up. She walked toward the group and smiled, intending to introduce herself to the two new members of the squad.

"Hi," she began, extending her hand toward the tall African American girl. "I'm Wendy."

"Janet," the girl said, smiling back. She reached out to shake Wendy's hand, but Kyle rudely walked between them with a couple of chairs and the whole group began to sit.

When they were settled, Janet turned in her seat to continue the conversation. But before she could say anything, Kyle looked over his shoulder and lifted his eyebrow. "Did you want something, Wendy?" he asked as if she were some pesky kid.

The smile froze on Wendy's face. Rachel's shoulders began to shake with laughter. Several people put their hands over their mouths to hide their smiles.

Some things never change, Wendy thought angrily. The South Beach Squad seemed determined to be as snobby and competitive this year as they had been last year.

"I wanted to say hello," Wendy said. "But I think I'll say good-bye instead."

"Good-bye, Wendy," they all chorused in a taunting tone before breaking into giggles at their own rudeness.

Wendy went back to her table, determined not to let them bring her down. This summer she had somebody to dance with, party with, and hang with. This summer she wasn't going to be lonely.

"Want to dance?"

Nina turned to see who'd asked her to dance. Her heart gave a pleased flutter when she saw a familiar handsome face. "Paul, right? From the surfboard rental stand?"

"You remember?"

"How could I forget?" she said with a flirtatious giggle. Paul's broad shoulders looked even broader in the light blue polo shirt he wore with pressed khaki shorts. The clothes and the short-clipped hair made him look very preppy. Nina found that somehow reassuring.

Ryan had conveyed the impression that Paul was maybe a little . . . *disreputable*. But nobody could have looked more clean-cut—or handsome—than Paul did now. "I'd love to dance," she answered, giving him her widest smile. She held out her hand and he took it, leading her out to the floor.

It was a fifties-style tune, and Nina loved partner dancing. Trouble was, her boyfriend, Bryan, didn't.

Paul did, though. It was apparent from the minute his hand settled confidently at her waist.

She never had any sense of being pushed or pulled, and she found herself effortlessly following him through a complicated set of steps.

"You're a great dancer," he said appreciatively.

"I was just thinking the same thing about you," she said as she twirled around. He caught her hand behind his waist, turned himself, and wound up face-to-face with her without ever missing a beat.

It was a short song, but by the end of it Nina felt as if she and Paul had been dancing together for years. "If they ever have a contest," she said, "I want you as my partner. Don't let anybody else sign you up."

Paul put one hand over his heart. "I'm all yours," he said with a half smile on his face. "That is, unless you already belong to somebody else."

Nine chewed her bottom lip and shook her braids back off her shoulders. The yellow beads clicked gaily. "Well . . . ," she muttered with a noncommittal smile.

Paul took her hand and pulled her toward the door. "Let's take a walk and you can tell me all about him."

Nina threw back her head and laughed at his brazenness, threading her arm through his and walking beside him. They walked down the pier toward the beach.

Once they reached the sand, she removed her white sandals with the chunky heels and carried them in her free hand.

"Now," Paul said. "Tell me who he is."

"His name is Bryan."

"And is he incredibly handsome, rich, and socially well connected?"

"No. He's incredibly intelligent and incredibly committed. He's working on Capitol Hill this summer."

Paul shook his head and clucked his disapproval. "Oh, he sounds like a very dull guy. Not your type at all. I'd forget all about him if I were you."

Nina giggled. It was so nice to be with someone who not only knew how to dance, but also knew how to flirt. "And concentrate on you?"

"Well, I'd probably be less work—from an intellectual standpoint. I'm not much of a student. But I *am* incredibly committed to having a good time. I'm a dedicated beach bum. You like to surf?" he asked suddenly.

"I love surfing. I also love snorkeling, parasailing, rowing, and waterskiing. Any water sport."

"Me too," Paul agreed with a laugh. "In fact, my ambition is to figure out how to spend my entire life on summer vacation. Scuba diving if possible." He arranged the collar of his polo shirt. "Come to think of it, that's sort of what I've been doing for the past couple of years now."

"Scuba diving?"

"Vacationing. Working on beaches and stuff like that. Scuba diving and surfing whenever I have the chance."

"Don't you go to school? What about next fall?"

Paul shrugged. "Next fall is a long way off. I've got plenty of time to decide what to do."

Nina debated with herself whether or not to press for more information and decided not to. Obviously Paul was no student. He was exactly what he described himself as being—a contented beach bum.

She wondered what it was like to be that kind of person. It was hard for her to imagine life without goals. Not that she was a total workaholic.

When she played, she played hard. But Nina definitely worked harder than she played. And all the guys she'd ever dated had been the same way.

"Wow! We've walked a long way," she said. "That's our house up there." She pointed to the three-story Victorian house. There was only one light on—in Elizabeth's room.

"Want to go back to the dance?" he asked. "Or shall I walk you home and try to talk you into kissing me good night?"

Nina tugged on his hand. "It's too early to go home. And too early to be talking about good-night kisses. Let's go back to the dance. Race you back," she challenged.

"You're on," Paul said, streaking ahead before she even had time to say "On your mark, get set, go."

"Hey!" she shouted. "That's cheating."

His only response was a laugh as he gestured to her to catch up.

"Jessica is, like, my very favorite name," a tall guy with a blond ponytail told her. "My name's Peter. I'm on the South Beach Squad."

Jessica smiled thinly. The guy was good-looking. But so were the other twenty-five guys who'd come on to her tonight. And at least ten of them had used the same line. Maybe they'd been out in the sun too long or something. Or maybe they were all using the same handbook.

She shifted her weight restlessly to her other foot and flicked the silky blond hair off her bare shoulder. She had been right about her outfit. The green dress made her stand out and it was killer effective—drawing attention even from the South Beach lifeguards.

Her eyes flickered over the crowd. The one face she was hoping to see was conspicuously absent. Ryan was nowhere to be seen.

The door opened, and she eagerly lifted her chin and set her mouth in its most provocative pout.

But much to her disappointment, it wasn't Ryan arriving, it was Nina coming back with some really good-looking guy.

Jessica watched them with a speculative eye as they wandered through the crowd, here and there speaking to someone they knew.

The guy was really hot. And Jessica could tell from the way Nina was tossing her head and smiling that she was interested. But she could also tell from the set of Nina's shoulders that she wasn't serious. Jessica wondered why. Bryan was a nice guy, but dull with a capital *D*.

Given a choice between Bryan and a hunk like that, Jessica would take the hunk. No contest.

Nina said something to the guy. He laughed. And then they parted. Nina caught Jessica's eye and threaded her way through the crowd in her direction. "Having fun?"

"Not really," Jessica answered.

"Let me see if I can guess why."

"It's not a secret," Jessica responded. "I was hoping Ryan would be here."

"Me too," Nina said with a sigh. "Why don't you go over to the lifeguard station and see if you

124

can get him to come to the dance for a little while? I think Ryan's a lot lonelier than he realizes."

Jessica looked around the room again and was startled to see a pair of deep blue eyes staring into hers. Ben!

He was surrounded by a group of girls, one of whom was resting her hand on his arm in the kind of flirtatious gesture Jessica knew so well.

Ben flashed her a crooked smile and lifted his glass as if to say . . . two can play at this game.

But Jessica wasn't interested in playing games with Ben. She looked away and flounced toward the door, determined to return with Ryan on her arm, wiping that smug smile off Ben's face forever.

Chapter
Eleven

Elizabeth sat on her bed and listened to the rhythmic boom of the surf outside. The curtains at the window billowed with every new ocean breeze and then gently deflated.

She shivered. It was getting chilly in the room. Elizabeth rolled off the bed, went to the window, and looked out. The ocean at night usually struck her as romantic. Tonight it just looked vast, overwhelming, and lonely. She couldn't remember the last time she'd felt so demoralized and incompetent. Her near-death experience in the ocean had left her shaken. She'd made a fool out of herself.

Ryan would have a hard time believing that for years, Elizabeth Wakefield had been considered the responsible, capable twin. And Jessica Wakefield had been considered scatterbrained, irresponsible, and undependable.

Not that Elizabeth cared what Ryan thought.
She didn't.

But she didn't like being misjudged. Not only by him, but by the other lifeguards. And Nina. *"Are we okay?"* Nina had asked.

No, they weren't okay. Elizabeth felt a stab of irritation. She kept waiting for Nina to tell her something like . . . *I had a talk with Ryan about you and told him what a superachiever you normally are. I told him that no matter what, I could always depend on you.*

But so far, all she'd heard from Nina—who was *supposed to be* her best friend and staunchest supporter—was that Ryan was right. And she was wrong.

Elizabeth was going to have to qualify for the squad just like everybody else. Whatever she'd done right in the past might as well have happened in another life for all the good it was doing her now.

She fell forward on the bed and groaned into her pillow. Nina was supposed to be on her side. Was this the behavior of a true best friend? Would a true best friend have put on tight white jeans and a sexy blouse and gone off to a dance when her bosom buddy was obviously bummed and down in the dumps? No.

Elizabeth sat up. "It's times like this you find out where you stand with people," she said out loud. She pulled a hooded sweatshirt on over her

T-shirt and shorts and went downstairs to the telephone.

Quickly she punched in Tom's number in Colorado. She needed a pep talk. Not to mention romantic conversation and compliments.

"Hello?" Finally! A voice instead of voice mail.

"Tom?"

"No. This is Frederick, his roommate. Tom's not in."

"This is his girlfriend, Elizabeth. Do you know what time Tom will be in?"

Frederick laughed. "I'm sorry, but I don't have any idea. We just finished our first week of classes and there's a major party in the radio and TV building lobby. Traditionally it goes on all night. Want me to leave a note for him to call you tomorrow?"

"Yes," Elizabeth said. "Yes. Please. I'll give you the number."

"What's your name again?"

"Elizabeth."

While Frederick jotted down her name and number, Elizabeth tried not to wonder why Tom's roommate didn't recognize her name. She also tried not to imagine Tom dancing the night away in the arms of some curvy brunette anchorperson from Denver.

"Tell him it's important," Elizabeth said, despising herself for sounding so clingy. "I really need to talk to him."

128

"I'm putting three exclamation points on the note," Frederick promised. Then he wished her good night and clicked off brusquely, obviously in a hurry to get to the party himself.

Elizabeth paced around the large, empty living room, trailing her fingers along the back of the blue leather recliner and the canvas-covered sofa.

Maybe separate vacations had been a mistake. When Tom had been accepted into the summer communications program, she'd considered applying herself. But then Nina had told her about Sweet Valley Shore. It had sounded like a whole lot more fun than spending the summer debating camera angles and the advantages of film versus tape.

Elizabeth had decided that she and Tom were adults, secure enough to spend their vacations separately without feeling threatened.

Ha!

They hadn't been apart a week and already Elizabeth was picturing Tom with some other girl. She pushed open the screen door and stepped out onto the front porch. The white foam shone in the moonlight. And faint music and laughter floated toward the house from the Sand Bar.

A tear began rolling down Elizabeth's cheek. Her hand flew up and fiercely wiped it away. *Cut it out!* she warned herself. *So what if you got off to a bad start. You just have to turn it around, that's all. Stay one step ahead of trouble and you'll be fine.*

She took some deep breaths and savored the salty air. What she needed was some downtime. Time to think. Time to reflect.

There was a thick paperback in the bottom of her duffel bag. She'd make herself a cup of tea, get back on her bed, and read until the others got home.

"Knock, knock!" Jessica said softly. She paused in the open door of the lifeguard station. Ryan stood inside, uncoiling a large section of rope.

He looked up and seemed surprised. "Hi," he said mildly.

"May I come in?"

"Sure."

Jessica stepped inside the lifeguard station, looked up and down at the shelves full of equipment, and smiled. "Nice place you got here."

"Actually my living quarters are in the back. And they're nothing to write *Architectural Digest* about."

She'd never seen him in anything but a bathing suit before. His faded jeans, chambray shirt, and boots made him look even taller and more broad shouldered than usual. And he was wearing glasses. Wire-rimmed aviator glasses.

"I didn't know you wore glasses," she said. She held out her hands. "May I?" It was a good excuse to move closer to him.

He removed the glasses and she put them on. Ryan's gorgeous face blurred.

Ryan laughed when she removed them. "I usually wear contacts." He put his glasses back on.

Being this close to him, and alone, gave Jessica a breathless feeling. And she felt the familiar fluttering sensation in her stomach that told her she had a major crush.

He eyed her from head to toe and then raised his brows. "You look nice. Are you going somewhere?"

"There's a dance at the Sand Bar. Everybody's there, including Nina. She asked me to come over and see if you wanted to join us."

Ryan smiled, as if he were really pleased. "Thanks. That's nice, but I've got a lot of stuff to do around here and . . ."

"Please don't say no," Jessica begged in her lightest, teasing tone. "You'll hurt my feelings."

He thought a moment, then put down the rope and looked her in the eye. "I wouldn't want to hurt the feelings of a beautiful girl and a great potential lifeguard. Let me get my keys."

A little thrill of victory raced up Jessica's spine as Ryan disappeared through the door that led to his room and then reappeared a few minutes later. They left the station, locked the door, and walked side by side up the beach to the brightly lit Sand Bar.

"So tell me about yourself," she said. It wasn't a very original line, but she knew from experience that if you could get a man to talk about himself, seventy-five percent of the battle was over.

"No. You tell me about Jessica," he countered in a bantering tone. "I want to hear what life is like as an identical twin."

"Oh, boy! That's a whole summer's worth of conversation."

"We've got all summer. So start talking."

Taking a big chance, she put her hand on his arm. When Ryan didn't pull away, Jessica linked her arm through his and kept up a light chatter all the way up the beach. By the time they reached the Sand Bar, Ryan was smiling and laughing. It was hard to believe he was the same man who could scowl so fiercely.

Once inside, Jessica looked around for Ben. She didn't see him and felt a slight flicker of disappointment. Ryan gently disengaged her arm and then put his large hand against her bare back, guiding her toward the bar. His hand felt warm and spanned the length between her shoulder blades.

"What would you like to drink?" he asked as they approached the crowded bar. He lifted his hand and caught the attention of the bartender.

"Sparkling water for me."

"Two sparkling waters," he told the bartender.

Jessica was surprised. Ryan was over twenty-one. Or at least he looked over twenty-one. It was odd that he didn't order a beer. The Sand Bar featured an extensive line of imported ales and lagers.

"And add a twist of lime, please," he added.

The young bartender nodded and reached toward the plastic dishes full of olives, orange slices, cherries, and various other drink garnishes.

When they had their drinks, they sauntered along the perimeter of the dance floor. Nina and the hunky guy were dancing to a funky reggae. When Nina spotted them, she waved happily.

Jessica waved back and gave her an imperceptible wink.

Ryan's head nodded up and down to the music.

"Want to dance?" Jessica asked boldly.

Ryan looked embarrassed. "I can't dance to this stuff," he said. "Let's wait for something simpler."

A few sips later the reggae song had ended and the strains of a familiar ballad elicited enthusiastic applause. "I remember this song," Jessica said. "It was popular when I was in high school."

"Now this is more my speed." He took Jessica's glass from her hand, set it on a table beside his own, and led her out onto the floor.

She lifted her arms and draped them loosely around his neck. He bent over and encircled her waist with his arms.

It felt good to be held, Jessica thought. She felt her eyes close, and almost involuntarily she laid her head against his broad chest. She felt his heart beating beneath his shirt and smiled. The irregular rhythm told her the attraction was mutual.

She tightened her arms and expected to feel his arms tighten around her waist and pull her closer. Instead they seemed to go slack, and he pulled away slightly.

Jessica loosened her embrace and looked down, a bit embarrassed. Maybe she was pushing things. She didn't want to come on too strong. It was still early in the summer. They had the lifeguard tryouts to get through. Maybe getting too close now would put him in an awkward position professionally.

Determined to act as if nothing had passed between them, she took a step back, put her hands on his shoulders, and continued to sway to the music with a smile on her face.

He smiled back, and she relaxed a little. "Did you go to many dances last summer?"

Ryan shook his head. "No. I usually go to bed early and get up early." The song was coming to an end, and he released her before the last note had sounded. "Thanks for coming by and getting me out for a drink and a dance. But I've got a lot to get done in the morning, so I'm going to say good night now." He bent over and kissed her cheek. "Have fun, and I'll see you tomorrow."

The next thing she knew, Ryan was gone.

"Hey!" a sharp voice behind Winston said.

Winston stood at the bar, holding a five-dollar bill in the air. He was trying to get the attention of the bartender.

"Hey!" Something about the undercurrent of irritation made Winston realize that the *hey* was directed at him.

He looked around and jumped slightly. Pedro Paloma stood right behind him, watching Winston with an expression that looked less than friendly.

Pedro took Winston's elbow and pulled him aside so they could speak. Up close, Pedro Paloma looked just like he did on Wendy's poster—except that he wasn't in the requisite singing-star pose. Nonetheless, Winston reflected, if he were a girl, he'd definitely be doing some serious swooning right now.

But he wasn't a girl. He was just a guy in the Sand Bar. A guy with no particular claim to fame.

So why was Pedro Paloma talking to him?

"Aren't you the guy who brought a walking tour to my house today?" Pedro asked.

Oh. Winston sucked his upper lip for a moment, debating with himself whether or not to lie. Captain Feehan had thrown a bunch of extremely alarming phrases around. Like "trespassing" and "damaging private property."

"Never mind. I know you are. Not many guys around here wear red propeller beanies."

Winston's eyes involuntarily looked upward as if to assure himself that it was indeed his headgear that was the subject of discussion.

Pedro Paloma smiled. It was a nice smile. Not the smile of a guy who was mad and ready to call

135

the cops. And Pedro didn't look like a rich and powerful local landowner ready to crush Winston beneath his heel. He looked like an ordinary guy in a gray boat-neck sweater and black jeans with boots. His long hair was pulled back in a braid, and Winston noticed a tiny cross hanging from a gold earring.

Winston also noticed that a lot of women were stealing looks in their direction. And they weren't sneaking peeks at his propeller beanie. Okay. Maybe calling Pedro an "ordinary guy" was a stretch. Not too many ordinary guys got that much attention from women. And very few "ordinary guys" his age had their own beach condo and red Porsche.

Pedro dug into the pocket of his jeans and pulled out a wad of money. "Look, I know everybody's got to make a living. But I'd really appreciate it if you'd take my place off the tour. Would a couple of hundred dollars convince you?"

Winston's jaw fell open. Two hundred bucks to take his house off the tour. Pedro Paloma was obviously unaware that Captain Feehan had already pulled the plug on his tour business. This would be the easiest two hundred bucks Winston had ever made.

He smiled. Two hundred bucks added to what he'd made that afternoon would put him in the clear for the first month.

Of course, it wasn't really honest . . . but . . .

Across the room he caught a glimpse of Wendy's profile as she watched the dancers from a table near the floor. A sudden brainstorm caused Winston to clutch convulsively at Pedro's sleeve. "Come here," he said, insistently pulling the singer behind a knot of people so they couldn't be seen.

"Okay. Okay," Pedro said. "Three hundred dollars."

Winston waved his money away. "No. No. This isn't about money."

"Four hundred."

"No."

Pedro ran his hand back over his hair in a gesture of helpless frustration. "Look, man, I'm not trying to pull the big star routine, but it's kind of unnerving to open the door to get the paper and have a crowd of people staring at you before you've even had a cup of coffee."

Winston wet his lips, trying to figure out how to articulate the plan that was forming in his brain.

"For a guy in a propeller beanie, you drive a hard bargain," Pedro marveled. "Five hundred dollars. That's my last offer."

"I don't want your money," Winston insisted hoarsely.

"Come on . . ."

"I mean it," Winston said. He pushed Pedro's hand away.

"You mean you'll take my house off the tour for nothing?"

"Well . . . uh . . . no," Winston stuttered. "I want you to do something. Not for me. For somebody else. For a fan."

Pedro shrugged. "I have no problem with that. You want me to dedicate a song to somebody?"

Winston shook his head. "No." He pulled Pedro a little closer to the edge of the bar and pointed. "See that girl over there? The one in the green T-shirt with the shoulder-length brown hair?"

Pedro nodded. "You want me to send her an autographed picture?"

"I want you to take her out."

Pedro pulled his sleeve away from Winston and snorted, as if he thought Winston was nuts.

"I mean it," Winston said. "She's a great girl. Her name is Wendy. She was a lifeguard last year and probably will be again this year. And she thinks you're terrific."

"That's really nice. But I can't take out some girl I don't know just because . . ."

"I'd think about it seriously if I were you. Because if you say no, I might show up tomorrow with another twenty tourists who'll stake out your house until they get a glimpse of you."

Pedro's olive-skinned complexion paled slightly and he swallowed. "This is blackmail."

Winston shrugged just like Pedro had. "I have no problem with that."

Pedro's gaze wavered back and forth between Winston's face and Wendy's, as if he were trying to gauge how serious Winston was about this. He let out a defeated sigh and his heavy lids blinked his acquiescence. "What's her name again?"

"Wendy," Winston said happily. "You'll get along great. Trust me."

"What am I supposed to do?"

"Just go on over, introduce yourself, give her a little of the old Pedro Paloma charm, and ask her out."

An obstinate frown crossed Pedro's face.

"You'll thank me for it," Winston chirped.

Pedro shoved his beer bottle into Winston's hand and started through the crowd in Wendy's direction. "I doubt it," he said sourly.

Chapter
Twelve

"Looks like your boyfriend wasn't having a very good time."

Jessica bristled.

Ben grinned. "Don't get your feathers ruffled. I'm just teasing you." He flagged the bartender.

Jessica was leaning back against the bar, watching the dancers. She didn't even bother to answer Ben. She simply walked out the side door of the Sand Bar and onto the deck that overlooked the water. She really didn't feel like dealing with a heckler right now.

Much to her annoyance, Ben followed.

Still ignoring him, she leaned over a rail and stared down at the water that lapped around the wooden posts. The light from the moon beamed down on the water, creating a mirror, and her blond hair appeared almost white in the reflection.

Ben put his elbows on the rail and looked down. "I feel like I'm looking at a mermaid," he said.

Jessica didn't answer, and Ben cleared his throat. He seemed almost ill at ease. As if he were trying hard to think of something to say now that he'd decided to be pleasant.

"Want something to drink?" he asked.

She shook her head, letting her hair ripple and shimmer in the moonlit water below.

"Something to eat?"

This time she didn't even bother to shake her head. Her thoughts were too full of Ryan. She wondered why he had left. He liked her. Or at least he seemed to like her. What was she doing wrong? She mentally reviewed their entire relationship, from the moment he'd first spoken to her to now.

He had made the first move when he had complimented her reflexes. That had to be a good sign. Didn't it? Was she making progress? Or was Ryan taking two steps back for every one step forward?

Farther out, the surf was high and rough, and she could see whitecaps bursting in the distance.

She became aware of the sound of Ben's voice and realized he had been talking to her. Bored and impatient, Jessica turned. "What?" she asked irritably, wishing he would leave her alone with her thoughts. What was with this guy anyway? He ragged on her. He put her down. He was totally obnoxious. And now he was trying to get on her good side.

"I was asking you if you knew what the weather was going to be like tomorrow," he repeated—as if he were talking to somebody who was deaf.

"How should I know?" she snapped.

The cocky grin faded, but didn't waver. His blue eyes flashed angrily. "This may come as a surprise to you, but weather is a subject of ongoing interest to people in the lifeguard profession." His tone was even more cutting and sarcastic than usual. "And the way you'd know what the weather is supposed to be like is by looking in the newspaper. You do know what a newspaper is, don't you? It's black and white and read all over? Or do you still get most of your vital information about life from comic books and fashion magazines?"

Jessica stared at him through half-closed eyes. "You know what your problem is?"

"What?"

"You're jealous."

He let out a derisive snort.

"You're jealous of Ryan."

"Why would I be jealous of Ryan?"

"Because he and I are a sure thing," she said, hoping in her heart that she was telling the truth. "And you're making, like, no progress whatsoever."

He laughed nastily. "Some people have imaginary friends. Some people even have imaginary pets. You've got an imaginary boyfriend. If you ever decide you want something a little more tangible, you know where to find me."

Jessica's eyes narrowed dangerously. She was getting ready to kick him, but he was too fast. With an amused chuckle, he turned and began sauntering toward the steps that led to the beach.

"Good night," he called out, his voice sounding faint over the evening wind.

Jessica watched him walk away until his white T-shirt had disappeared into the night completely. "I'll show you," she vowed. "If it takes me all summer, I'll wipe that smile right off your face."

The sound of heavy clogs on the wooden boards of the dock interrupted her vengeful thoughts, and she gasped.

Rachel, the tall, sultry captain of the South Beach Squad, stood only a few yards away. She wore a white tank top, and her thumbs were hitched in the pockets of her low-slung denim shorts. They hung from her hips, revealing a wide expanse of flat, tanned tummy.

Her almond eyes stared malevolently at Jessica. It was the same look that Jessica had seen three days ago when she'd thrown the Frisbee right at her. "I want to talk to you," she said without preamble.

"About . . . ?"

"About Ben."

Jessica cocked her head in surprise. "What about him?"

"Stay away from him," she warned.

Jessica could only laugh. If Rachel had her eye on Ben, she was welcome to him.

Apparently Rachel misinterpreted her response. Rather than reading affirmation, she must have read it as a challenge. "I mean it," Rachel said ominously. She took several steps in Jessica's direction.

The clacking sound of her shoes sounded aggressive and businesslike, and the next thing Jessica knew, Rachel had grabbed a handful of her hair.

"Let me go," Jessica shouted in outrage.

"You bet," Rachel agreed in a genial tone.

Rachel kicked at Jessica's ankle with her wooden shoe and at the same time gave her shoulder a savage shove.

Jessica let out a scream of alarm that hardly had time to pierce the night air before she was submerged in cold ocean water and surrounded by the slimy seaweed that collected around the piers.

Jessica kicked fiercely and broke the surface, sputtering with rage. "How dare you?" she shouted.

Rachel leaned over the rail and laughed. "Don't mess with me," she warned. "And don't mess with Ben, either."

In spite of her dress Jessica managed to kick her way to the ladder and climb back up on the pier.

But Rachel was gone.

Jessica debated with herself for a few seconds over whether or not to go back into the Sand Bar and have it out with Rachel. She decided against it.

Jessica was a mess. And since nobody had witnessed the incident, Rachel could deny the whole thing and then Jessica would look like a fool.

Her shoes were ruined, and she angrily threw them off the dock and into the water. Then she ran down the steps to the beach and headed for the house.

144

Rachel doesn't have anything to worry about, she thought angrily. *The only interest I have in Ben is in tearing his head off and using it for shark bait.*

Wendy watched Rachel swagger through the crowd, swinging her thin hips and leading with her generous bust. Men went nuts over Rachel, and Rachel knew the effect she had. Wendy watched male heads turn and follow her progress through the crowded nightspot.

I wonder what it's like to look like that? Wendy thought. Once. Just once it would be nice to look like somebody who at least commanded enough respect so that obnoxious people like the South Beach Squad would grace her with a smile and even say hello.

"Hello."

Wendy looked up and felt her heart skip a beat. Pedro Paloma stood at the edge of her table, smiling right at her. His braid had fallen in front of his shoulder, and his dark brows formed a dramatic arch over the large brown eyes fringed with thick lashes.

Her mouth opened and closed a few times, but she couldn't seem to make any sound come out.

"We haven't met," Pedro said, "but I've seen you at my concerts several times." He held out his hand. "My friends call me Pedro."

Wendy's hand floated up and rested briefly in his. "I'm Wendy," she managed to squeak.

"Mind if I sit down?" he asked.

"No," she said so quickly, it practically came out a shout.

He pulled out the empty chair next to her and sat down, leaning both elbows on the table and gazing at her with frank and friendly interest. "When did you develop an interest in my music?" he asked.

The first time I saw you walk into a club, she thought. But she couldn't say that. "Oh, you know . . . ," she improvised. "I started hearing it on the radio and . . ." She shrugged. "I became a fan."

"What other kinds of music do you like?" he asked.

"Classical, mainly baroque. Sixties rock. And contemporary jazz."

"Contemporary jazz is cool," he said. "Have you been to the Deep Blue Note?"

She shook her head.

"It's a coffee shop down the beach. They play progressive jazz over the sound system. It's not live, but it sounds pretty good. Would you like to join me sometime?"

Wendy wondered if her jaw thumped when it hit the wooden tabletop. "Are you asking me out on a date?" she gasped.

He smiled and laughed kindly. "I guess I'm not doing a very good job if you're not sure. Yes. I'm asking you out on a date."

"Why?" Only after the word had involuntarily escaped her lips did Wendy realize how rude and uncool it sounded. But she couldn't think of one reason in the world why this incredibly gorgeous and very popular performer would want to go out with her.

The blunt question seemed to take him completely by surprise. He blinked several times and nervously wet his lips. "Ahhhhh," he began.

"I'm sorry. That was a really uncool response." She covered her face with her hands. "Wow! I'm so embarrassed."

He laughed and pulled her hands from her face. "I'd like to go out with you because I'm an egomaniac. If I go out with a fan, I know we're going to spend the whole night talking about me."

That broke the tension, and they both laughed. Pedro reached into his back pocket and removed a piece of paper and a stub of pencil. "Give me your number so I can call you and make a plan."

Wendy gave him her number and couldn't help sneaking a peek in the direction of the South Beach Squad. She could see big blond Danielle watching. Danielle nudged Rachel, and Rachel looked over at the table. Rachel's brows flew up in surprise and she shrugged, as if to say, *Who knows what that's all about.*

Then Rachel said something to her friends and there was a burst of laughter. But Wendy didn't blush or get mad. Who cared what the South Beach Squad did or didn't do? Who cared if they said hello? Who cared what they thought?

The only person whose opinion she cared about was Pedro Paloma's. And he seemed to think she was just fine.

*　　　*　　　*

"What are you doing out here by yourself?" Ben asked, walking up the beach toward her.

Elizabeth was in front of the house at the water's edge, with the hood of her sweatshirt pulled over her head against the chilly evening breeze. She shoved her hands deeper into her pockets and kicked at the sand with the toe of her sneaker. "I got bored reading," she answered honestly.

"Why don't you go to the Sand Bar? That's where all the action is."

"If that's where the action is, how come you're home already?"

Ben shrugged. "I've had enough. Tell me something. What's with your sister?"

Elizabeth gave Ben a long look. He seemed like a nice guy, but he was a little too intense and sarcastic. Not exactly Jessica's type.

"Think she'll actually land Ryan?" he blurted before she'd had a chance to respond to his first question.

There was no hint of mockery in his voice now. It was a serious question. And for the first time he sounded as if he regarded it as a real possibility.

"I don't know," she said softly.

Ryan might be rude, dictatorial, and authoritarian, but there was no doubt that he was nice to Jessica. And he was bringing out all her best qualities. Jessica was taking an interest in training. She was excelling. And she was cheerful.

On the other hand, Ryan *disliked* Elizabeth.

148

Elizabeth wasn't used to being disliked. It made her uncomfortable. It shook her self-confidence. And it was affecting her ability to think clearly.

"I'm going in," Ben said. "'Night."

"Good night," Elizabeth responded softly.

She could hear Paloma Perro barking inside the house as Ben ran jauntily up the steps. A greeting from Ben seemed to reassure him, and then the screen door shut with a bang that reverberated throughout Elizabeth's whole body.

The house, with its few feeble lights, seemed dwarfed by the vast dark night and the endless ocean. Elizabeth began walking away from the faint sounds of music and laughter coming from the Sand Bar. They were making her feel depressed. Maybe if she got far enough down the beach, she wouldn't hear the noise.

The lifeguard station was dark, and as she walked past the main tower she came to a startled halt when she saw a tall figure in jeans and a shirt standing in the sand, looking out at the water.

Ryan!

"Hello," she said cautiously.

He turned his head and studied her for a long moment. She couldn't help thinking how good he looked in clothes. She was so used to seeing him in his red trunks. The wind was picking up speed and his chambray shirt billowed open, revealing the upper part of his chest. His skin in the moonlight was a golden brown. "What are you doing out here?" he asked.

"I'm allowed to take a walk by myself, aren't I?" she responded, irritated to be asked that for the second time tonight. She tried to make it sound like a joke, but she could hear the antagonistic note in her voice.

Apparently so did he.

Ryan scratched his chin, thinking. "Listen, Elizabeth. I think I've been too hard on you. And I'm sorry."

An apology was the last thing Elizabeth had expected. And he sounded like he meant it.

She took a deep breath. Maybe a frank discussion would clear the air and get things on a more even keel. "Why *are* you so hard on me?" she asked, making sure she didn't sound as if she were whining. "I'm not as irresponsible and stupid as you seem to think. In fact, most people consider me extremely capable, competent, and intelligent."

His eyebrows met over his nose and his contrite expression turned to a scowl. "*That's* why I'm so hard on you. Listen to yourself. You're exactly the kind of person I *don't* want on my squad. An overachiever. A hotdogger. Somebody so used to doing things right, they think they can't possibly screw up. People like you get so overconfident, they stop paying attention and do stupid things. And when they do, somebody gets hurt. Do me a favor. Think very hard about whether or not you're cut out for this job."

Ryan walked quickly up to the station, entered the front door, and closed it with a slam.

Elizabeth stood there, feeling as if she had been slapped. She could hardly breathe, she was so stunned. She could hardly move. It was as if her feet had turned to stone.

She'd never felt so unfairly misjudged in her whole life. She'd gotten off to a bad start with Ryan, and nothing she did would change his mind.

Why had she let Nina talk her into coming here? Why hadn't she gone to Colorado with Tom? She closed her eyes and wished with all her heart that he were here.

Tom loved her. He believed in her. And he didn't resent the fact that she was intelligent, competent, and an achiever.

A tear trickled down her cheek. This time she didn't wipe it away. She began running back toward the house, sobbing.

The light was on beneath Ben's door, but Jessica didn't bother to knock. She twisted the knob and shoved the door open so hard it bounced against the wall.

Ben lay on the bed, wearing a pair of track shorts and no shirt. A novel rested on his chest, and he looked up and whistled. "Wow! Looks like somebody went overboard."

Jessica stomped over to the bed, leaving a trail of wet, sandy footprints. Her green gauzy dress was still soaked and clung like a second skin. But she was too angry to feel modest.

"I've got something for you. From your girl-friend," she said angrily.

Ben sat up, and the hard stomach muscles rippled. "Oh, yeah? That's funny. I don't have a girl-friend."

Jessica flung a fistful of slimy black seaweed at his face. "Tell it to Rachel," she spat.

Ben laughed a high-pitched wheezing laugh as he clawed the slimy seaweed from his face. "Rachel always was a thoughtful person."

"Well, I have a thought for your pal Rachel. Tell her to stay away from me. And you stay away from me too."

With that she threw her other handful of sea-weed. It hit his chest with a satisfying smack.

Jessica turned on her heel and marched out, slamming the door behind her. As she climbed the stairs she could still hear Ben laughing.

The sound of his laughter made her even angrier. "I hate you, Ben," she muttered through clenched teeth. "I only wish you knew exactly how much."

Chapter
Thirteen

Nina moved nervously around the kitchen along with Elizabeth, Winston, and Wendy. The big day had arrived—final cuts for the lifeguard squad would be announced today. She grabbed a knife and was putting two pieces of bread in the toaster when the phone ran. "I'll get it," she said quickly.

But she was too late.

Elizabeth, Winston, and Wendy stampeded out of the kitchen in the direction of the living room.

"I'm sure it's Tom," Elizabeth cried, stepping over a chair to get past Nina. "I left a message for him three nights ago."

"No, it's not," Winston insisted, leaping in front of her. "It's Denise. She promised to call as soon as she got settled."

"Doesn't anyone realize it might be for me?" Wendy asked angrily.

Jessica dove out of the downstairs bathroom

and put her hand on it first. "It's probably Ryan, for me," she said, giving Ben a smug smile as he appeared in the doorway of his room.

Nina arrived in the living room in time to watch Jessica grab the phone and compose herself by taking a deep breath. "Hello?" she said in a low, melodious voice.

It had been two days since the dance at the Sand Bar. The group had had two more days of hard drilling. Two days of tension and arguments. And two days of waiting for the phone to ring.

Denise hadn't called Winston. Tom hadn't called Elizabeth. And Paul hadn't called Nina.

Nina had talked to her boyfriend Bryan last night. Hearing his voice had made her feel moderately guilty about wishing that Paul would call. Still, guilt or no guilt, Paul was gorgeous and fun. And she looked forward to hearing from him again.

The entire group watched Jessica, faces tense with suspense. Jessica listened for a moment, then frowned. "No. There's no Bernie here. You have a wrong number." Jessica slammed down the phone, and everybody groaned.

"What a bummer way to start the day," Winston moaned.

Elizabeth walked back into the kitchen. "We need to get an answering machine," she said. "I know Tom's going to call me today when I'm not around."

Winston plucked a grape from the bunch in the middle of the table. "Ditto Denise."

Nina chewed on a cuticle. She didn't want to say anything about Paul in front of the others. She wasn't serious about him. But she wouldn't mind talking to him.

They all filed back into the kitchen, and Ben let out a crack of laughter as he opened a bag of doughnuts and poured himself some coffee. "What is this? Camp Lovesick? Look at you people. You're pathetic. Miles of beach and surf and you're sitting here waiting for the phone to ring. Get a life."

"Why don't you show us how?" Jessica snapped. "If it works out well for you, then maybe we'll all give it a try."

Nina stared at the demoralized group and reached a conclusion. "Ben's right," she said, slapping a palm down on the table. "We've got to pull ourselves together. We've got a job to do."

"*If* we make the cut," Winston reminded her. "Which is by no means certain. At least for some of us."

"Stop being negative," Nina barked, feeling more nervous than she liked to let on. Winston was right. None of them was guaranteed a spot on the squad. There were a lot of good, strong swimmers who had done very well over the last few days. The group assembled in the kitchen had their work cut out for them.

Paloma Perro nudged her leg under the table. "I want everybody to think positive." Nina reached over, snatched the doughnut from Ben's hand, and fed it to Paloma. She heard it disappear in a gulp.

After a great deal of elaborate smacking, Paloma's nose appeared in her lap and his large, soulful eyes rolled up, begging for another one. "That's it," she told him. "And that's it for you guys, too. No doughnuts. Eat a yogurt and a five-grain bagel," she instructed. "Sugar will give you a quick boost, but it'll let you down fast. And you're going to need all the energy you can muster today."

She saw the group begin to sit up a little straighter. "No more slinking around waiting for the phone to ring. I want everybody to eat a balanced breakfast. Then we're going to do a quick warm-up workout. And then . . . we're going to report to the lifeguard station."

Nina stood and lifted her orange juice glass. "I just want everybody here to know that I have nothing but faith in all of your abilities." She glowered comically. "If anybody flakes out, poops out, weaks out, or chickens out, I will take it as a personal insult. Is that clear?"

"Ma'am. Yes, ma'am," they all shouted as if they were in the military.

"Okay, then, a toast."

They all stood and lifted their glasses.

"Good luck to everyone," Nina said. "Now eat up and let's go kick some butt."

They clinked their glasses, and Paloma Perro put his paws up on the table and barked.

* * *

Jessica pulled the leg holes of her bathing suit down over the tiny curve of her bottom and shrugged her shoulder, adjusting the strap on her buoy. This wasn't her sexiest bathing suit, but it was the most utilitarian. She could move in it. And job one was to get on the squad. Looking good could wait.

Once she was on the squad, she'd be in almost daily contact with Ryan. A little time. A little tan. A little bikini. She'd have him in the palm of her hand. No problem.

Just as Nina had predicted, the number of candidates had dwindled every day as people realized exactly how hard and demanding the job was going to be.

Still hanging in there were Marcus Collier, a short, muscular junior from USC, who wore his blond hair in an old-fashioned crew cut, and Paula McFee, a sophomore from UVA who shared a house with Kerry Janowitz. Kerry looked tall and lanky like Winston, but he seemed to have incredible strength and stamina.

Also assembled were a guy everybody called Jocko, a group of girls who had drilled with them every day for the last three days, and four guys whose names Jessica never could keep straight.

The group had just finished the written test on topography, hazards, and procedures. And now Ryan was going over the agenda for the rest of the tryouts.

They would all have to complete a series of

timed relays and demonstrate CPR proficiency.

Jessica's fingers noticed that the strap on her buoy was frayed. As unobtrusively as possible she slipped away from the group, ran into the lifeguard station, and exchanged it for another one.

She hurried back outside. But before she had taken two steps, something in the water caught her eye. Could it be a swimmer? The beach wasn't open for swimming yet.

She squinted and lifted her hand to block the sun. The unmistakable wave of a hand set her feet in motion like an electric shock.

Jessica ran to the water, high-stepping over the waves until she was thigh deep. She dove and started stroking, knifing through the water, propelled by adrenaline.

Just as she had been taught in lifesaving, she kept her eye on the target, determined not to lose track of the swimmer in the rough water.

As soon as she got within range she threw the buoy. Her heart turned over and thumped with relief when it hit the water within inches of his grasp.

"Hold on!" she shouted as he clutched the flotation device.

"It's my leg," the young man choked. "I can't kick. I ca—"

"Don't try to talk," she said. "Tell me on the shore." She began swimming back toward the shore. The drag of the buoy slowed her down a little, but the drilling had paid off. She was amazed at the amount of strength her arms possessed.

She had only gone a few feet when she saw Ryan approaching with his own buoy. He was a strong swimmer, and in a matter of seconds he had reached them.

"We're okay," Jessica gasped.

Ryan nodded. "You're doing great. I'll just swim along beside you until we get to shore."

Jessica continued kicking and stroking. As soon as they hit the shallow water Ryan helped the young man to his feet and Jessica shucked off the shoulder strap of the buoy and reeled it in.

The young man limped painfully. "It's my knee," he explained. "I hurt it last year playing football, and sometimes it goes out on me."

Ryan ducked beneath the young man's arm, draped it over his shoulder, and carried him up on the beach. Very carefully he helped him sit down. Everyone gathered around and watched quietly while Ryan cupped the guy's chin in his large palm and studied his eyes, looking for signs of shock.

After a few moments he seemed satisfied. He gave the young man an encouraging smile. "You're okay," he said in a warmer voice than Jessica had ever heard him use. "But what were you doing out there in the water? The beach isn't open for swimming yet. It won't be until Saturday."

The guy began to shiver, and Nina draped a towel over his shoulders, rubbing his arms. He gave Ryan a worried look. "I just wasn't thinking, I guess. Really stupid, huh?"

Jessica wondered if Ryan was going to chew him out. "Are you by yourself?" he asked kindly.

"I'm staying with friends. About a mile down the beach," he answered.

Ryan straightened up. "Nina. The keys to the dune buggy are in the lifeguard station by my bed. Take this guy back to his house, will you?" He turned to Jessica. "Jessica, you come with me. I'll show you how to fill out an incident report in your logbook. Every lifeguard has to keep a logbook."

"But I'm not a lifeguard yet," Jessica reminded him.

"Yes, you are," he said. "That was the most amazing tryout I've ever seen. Everybody else hang loose till I come back."

"Nice work, Jess," Elizabeth said quietly, giving her a gentle hug. "You should get a medal."

"Thanks," Jessica said. *I don't want a medal,* she thought. *I want the prize. And I think I'm about to get it.*

Jessica couldn't keep the corners of her mouth from turning up in a proud smile. She'd done a great job. She'd earned Ryan's respect. And the others were gazing at her with envy and admiration.

She caught Ben giving her a crooked grin.

She was in such a good mood, she even grinned back.

160

Chapter Fourteen

"I'm often asked, how do you know when some-body's in trouble or just horsing around?" Ryan said, addressing the group while Nina swam out fifty yards.

Elizabeth nervously adjusted the strap of her buoy. They were executing mock rescues, and it was her turn.

"Believe me," Ryan continued, "when you see somebody in trouble, you'll know it. You recog-nize the signs. The hands. The look on the face. Mainly you know they're really in trouble because they're not screaming very much. Screaming is work. It takes a lot of strength. And they're fight-ing for their lives."

Elizabeth shivered. She knew from firsthand experience how right he was.

They heard a shout. It was the signal from Nina that she was ready.

"Okay, Elizabeth. You've just spotted a victim. What do you do?" Ryan instructed.

Elizabeth pushed off the sand and ran to the water, stepping over the surf. She could hear screams and yells of encouragement from the beach as she breasted the waves.

She was making good time, and she felt calm and in control. Soon she was close enough to see Nina's face.

"Help," Nina squeaked in a comic voice. "Help me."

Just as they had been taught she stayed out of Nina's reach and tossed her the buoy. "Stay calm. I'm a lifeguard. If you'll relax and trust me, I'll get you to shore," she said, feeling a little silly as she delivered the scripted reassurance speech.

Nina grinned and made a funny face as she clutched the buoy. "Are there any sharks out here?" she asked.

Elizabeth laughed and got a mouthful of water. "Please don't make me laugh," she begged. "Or I'll goof up."

She turned like a dolphin in a harness and began swimming back. When they got close to shore, Elizabeth helped Nina to the sand.

Everybody applauded. It had been a textbook rescue. No snags. No problems.

Elizabeth smiled broadly, then noticed that Ryan was scribbling in his book, a frown on his face.

"You forgot something important," he said to Elizabeth.

Elizabeth felt her face freezing.

"What's the first thing you're supposed to do when you see a victim?" he asked.

She closed her eyes and groaned. "Signal somebody that I'm going in."

"Show me the signal."

Elizabeth lifted her arms and crossed them.

Ryan nodded. "This is important. Don't ever go in without letting another lifeguard know. *A*— you might need their help. *B*—somebody needs to cover your section of the beach. Winston, you're up next."

Elizabeth bit her lip nervously. Failing to signal that she was going in had been a major oversight. Had she just blown it?

She tried to catch Nina's eye, but Nina had already turned and started swimming back out, preparing for the next rescue.

"Stay calm," Winston told Nina. "I'm a lifeguard and . . . whoaaa!" he cried as the buoy slipped off his shoulder.

Nina, still clutching the buoy, began drifting away.

Winston paddled furiously in her direction, trying to grab the cord or the strap.

"Winston!" Nina cried. "How could you do that?"

163

A wave rose over their heads, and Winston went below the surface to escape the noise and commotion of the break. Beneath the water he felt the churn and tug of the current. When he surfaced, the ocean pulled him several feet away from Nina.

"Come back here and save me," she shouted angrily.

"I'm trying," Winston yelped, flipping onto his back and windmilling his arms. It was his best stroke.

"You're going in the wrong direction. I'm over here. Lose the backstroke."

Winston flopped over, looking right and left for Nina.

"Back here."

He twirled around. "Ah! There you are," he said happily.

"Hurry up," she urged. "This is timed, you know."

Winston's heart began to pound nervously. "Quit pressuring me," he said. "You're making me too nervous to save you."

Another wave rose up and lifted Nina. "Winston!" she shouted. "Winston. Save me! Save me right now or I'm going to kill youoooooooo. . . ."

But Winston watched helplessly as the wave gathered speed and momentum and sent Nina surfing toward the beach on his buoy.

"The timed ins and outs count for a lot,"

Wendy whispered to Winston, trying to sound encouraging. "You were really fast on those."

He sat beside her on the beach with a glum face. "If you say so."

"You did really well on the CPR."

Winston sighed wearily, ran a hand through his still damp curls, and reached for a towel.

Wendy patted his hand and then drew up her knees and rested her head on them. She'd done well. Almost everyone had done well. But almost everybody had made some mistakes, too. It was going to be a close competition.

The group sat on the beach in tense silence, waiting for Ryan to emerge from the lifeguard station with the results.

The door opened. "Come on," Wendy said, springing to her feet. "Let's go get the good news."

Elizabeth swallowed nervously and joined the small group of people who stood in a circle around Ryan. He held a clipboard and he wore sunglasses. It was impossible to read his face behind the mirrored lenses. "Nina! As I'm sure you already know, you're on the squad."

Elizabeth applauded along with everybody else.

"Wendy! You're back. But no practical jokes this year or you're history. Get it?"

Wendy saluted and then grinned. Next to her Winston's face wore a tight, nervous look. She turned to him and whispered something. He nodded.

Elizabeth knew Wendy was whispering words of encouragement, but Elizabeth had the sinking feeling that it was a waste of time. Winston had not distinguished himself.

Her stomach clenched. Her own status wasn't all that certain either. It was too soon to start feeling sorry for Winston. She might need her energy to feel sorry for herself.

Ryan consulted the list in his hand and pushed his sunglasses up on his nose. "Also on the Sweet Valley Shore Squad are Jessica, Marcus, Paula, Ben, Kerry, and . . ."

Elizabeth held her breath. There was only one more spot. She knew she was the most qualified candidate. But Ryan didn't like her. He'd made that plain. He'd told her he didn't want her on the squad. This wasn't a democracy. If he didn't want her on his team, he didn't have to hire her.

"Elizabeth," he finished.

"What?" Elizabeth whispered to Kerry, who was standing next to her. "Did he say my name?"

Unfortunately she didn't whisper softly enough because Ryan turned his mirrored sunglasses in her direction. She might not be able to see his eyes, but she could *feel* his glare. "Yes. I said your name. Are you awake?"

Elizabeth couldn't tell whether he expected an answer or not. So she said nothing. There was a long and uncomfortable pause.

Ryan cleared his throat. "Let me make it clear

that if I'm not satisfied with the attitude, aptitude, or performance of any lifeguard, I have the right to terminate your employment immediately."

A hot, humiliated, and angry flush crept up Elizabeth's neck to her ears. Obviously that remark was for her benefit.

"Everybody who didn't make it this summer, I want to thank you for trying so hard. Please come back again next year and have a great summer whatever you do."

As the dismissed candidates disbursed, Nina turned to Elizabeth and smacked her hand in a hearty high five. "Good for us. We made it. We all made it. This is absolutely fantastic."

Elizabeth looked over Nina's shoulder and saw Wendy walking beside Winston. Winston's head was hanging unhappily, and Wendy was talking earnestly. "We didn't all make it," Elizabeth reminded Nina.

Nina looked over at Winston and grimaced. "Yeow! This is going to be hard. Come on. Let's go see what we can do to make him feel better."

Elizabeth and Nina jogged over to join Winston. "Winston. Don't feel bad," Elizabeth begged.

Winston ran a hand through his loose curls. "How can I not feel bad? I'm the only one in the house who didn't make the squad. I'm the only one in the house who doesn't have a job. And something tells me that when next month's rent is due, I'll be the only one in the house who doesn't have a bed."

"We wouldn't kick you out," Nina protested. "Don't be ridiculous."

"And besides," Wendy said. "You have your tour business. Right?"

"Well . . . according to Captain Feehan, I don't have the right kind of license. I may have to knock off the tours for a while."

Elizabeth had known Winston long enough to know when he wasn't telling the truth. And he wasn't telling the truth now. But that was his business.

"Ryan's calling us back," Marcus said, joining them. "He wants to hand out the assignments for today."

"Look, Winston, don't worry," Elizabeth assured him. "We'll work something out."

Winston smiled thinly. "Sure. You guys go ahead. I'll just be on the beach catching some Z's. If you see me drowning or anything, swim out and say hello."

Elizabeth laughed, squeezed his shoulder, and then trotted after Nina and joined the group outside the lifeguard station.

Ryan gave them all a stern look. "May I have your attention, please?"

The group assembled around Ryan fell silent. "The most important thing I need to tell you guys . . . is that there's a bonfire and cookout tonight for all beach employees in the area. Attendance is mandatory. Tower Six on South Beach is the location."

The group laughed and applauded. "The next thing is that since next Saturday is the first day of Memorial Day weekend, let's get warmed up and ready for the crowds by getting familiar with the routines and working with each other. Ben, you and Marcus go down to the edge of the beach and patrol that area. There are a lot of whirlpools around the jetty and somebody needs to be posted there at all times."

Ryan handed them each a whistle and a T-shirt. Grinning proudly, the two guys pulled them on, draped the whistles over their necks, and ran athletically toward their post.

"Kerry and Paula, go over the equipment list in the station. Make sure everything's there and make sure it works." He handed them T-shirts and whistles.

"Nina. Make sure we have enough logbooks and get one set up for everybody. Jessica, you can work with me. Wendy and Elizabeth, you're on dog duty."

"What?" Elizabeth exclaimed.

He disappeared inside the lifeguard station, then reappeared with two implements that looked like dust-pans attached to a broomsticks. Pooper-scoopers.

"Dogs are prohibited on the beach," Ryan

explained patiently, handing each girl a scooper. "If you see somebody with a dog, tell them the dog is not supposed to be on the beach. If you see a dog with no person, call animal control. They'll send somebody to pick it up and take it to the shelter. If you see dog doo, clean it up." He held out a T-shirt and whistle.

Elizabeth paused for a moment, seriously debating whether or not to quit right now.

She was spared the decision. Wendy reached out and took both T-shirts and whistles from him. "Will do," she said cheerfully.

Jessica stood beside Ryan. Her face betrayed nothing. But a quiver in her neck told Elizabeth that she was exerting tremendous effort not to laugh.

"Good luck. If you have any problems at all, blow the whistle or flag Captain Feehan." Ryan gave them a brisk nod and then began walking down the beach with Jessica.

Elizabeth and Wendy exchanged a glance.

"Dog duty! Not exactly what you'd call the glamorous part of lifeguarding," Wendy cracked, pulling the T-shirt on over her head.

"He hates me," Elizabeth groaned.

"I'm beginning to think he does," Wendy agreed cheerfully.

Wendy idly flipped the pooper-scooper as they walked, making a rhythmic clatter. Her hair was pulled back in a rubber band, and she had donned a visor to keep the sun from scorching her nose. If Pedro Paloma *did* call, she didn't want him to see her looking like Rudolf the Red-Nosed Reindeer.

"This is the stupidest thing I've ever done," Elizabeth muttered. She poked moodily at the sand with her scooper. "Do you realize we've been walking up and down the beach for two hours?"

Wendy laughed. They had traversed the beach several times. So far, no dogs. And no dog poop. They were at the end of the beach now and approaching the pier that separated Sweet Valley Shore from South Beach.

They could hear the music from the jukebox in Hamburger Harry's, which was built out over the water off the pier. Several people sat at tables outside, eating hamburgers and nachos.

Several yards east was the boardwalk. Even though the beach wasn't open for swimming, crowds of people were surging up and down the boardwalk, visiting the shops and restaurants. There were also a lot of people sunbathing in the afternoon warmth.

Hot Dog Howie carts dotted the beach along the boardwalk. "Hot dogs!" the vendors shouted. "Howie's hot dogs!"

Wendy watched a young mother hand her two kids some money. Then the two little boys ran toward the cart with the crisp green dollar bills. Her stomach rumbled. She was hungry herself. And glad their shift would be over soon.

"Not only is it stupid, it's boring," Elizabeth added.

"In the lifeguard business boring is better than exciting," Wendy soothed, wishing Elizabeth would quit complaining. "When things get exciting, it usually means somebody's drowning."

"That's true. But there's boring and then there's *boring*."

"Uh-oh," Wendy said. "Ridicule approaching at twelve o'clock." The South Beach Squad was jogging in a pack, coming toward them from the other side of the pier. "I think they're heading for a hot dog."

"Maybe they'll just ignore us," Elizabeth said.

Wendy steeled herself. "Don't count on it."

There were several guffaws and snickers as the group passed. Wendy pointed at the ground. "Watch where you step," she shouted in alarm.

It was her turn to snicker when Kyle and Danielle practically tripped over their own feet in an effort to avoid the nonexistent dog doo.

Elizabeth laughed reluctantly.

The group came to a stop and muttered resentfully.

"Very funny," Danielle said.

Rachel lifted her lip and sneered. "Gosh, Wendy, keep up the good work and maybe Ryan will trust you with a little more responsibility."

The South Beach Squad guffawed loudly.

"Hey!" a male voice said sharply. "That wasn't

funny. I think you owe Wendy an apology. And I'd like to hear it. Now."

Wendy's mouth fell open when she realized that the stern admonition had come from Winston. He was standing a few yards away at one of Hot Dog Howie's carts.

He held a hot dog in one hand and a yellow plastic mustard dispenser in the other. He glared ferociously at Rachel and her crew.

Rachel, Kyle, Kristi, and Danielle all exchanged an amused glance.

Danielle turned to Winston. "And you *are* . . . ?" she said pretentiously.

"I *am* . . . offended and annoyed," Winston answered, mocking her affected manner.

"You are also skinny and nonathletic," Kyle reminded him. "And skinny, nonathletic guys take big chances when they pick arguments with South Beach."

Winston appeared completely unintimidated. "Oh?" he commented pleasantly. "I think you may have it backward, my good man. South Beach may be taking a big chance when it picks a fight with Winston Egbert."

"Winston," Wendy and Elizabeth both cried at once. "Don't—"

Winston sprang forward with a savage cry. He aimed the mustard right at Kyle. A loud, rude noise emanated from the plastic mustard canister and a stream of smelly yellow liquid spewed out, covering Kyle from nose to chin.

Wendy felt her shoulders rise to her ears and shake helplessly. "All right, Winston!" she managed to choke through her laughter.

"Why, you . . ." Kyle grabbed the red plastic ketchup canister from the top of the cart.

"Hey!" the hot-dog vendor protested.

But Kyle ignored him and aimed the ketchup at Winston with an extended arm. Winston backed up with his mustard arm extended while Kyle advanced with the ketchup.

"En garde," Wendy yelled as the two boys began a ludicrous fencing match.

Winston's attention was momentarily diverted and his aim went awry, spraying Tina, the petite Korean American. Tina let out an outraged shriek and grabbed a basket of chopped onions from the top of the cart. With a snarl she dove toward Winston and dumped the onions on his head.

"No fair," Wendy cried. "That's two against one." She pushed the vendor out of the way and grabbed a fistful of sauerkraut from one of the warm steam trays. "Take that!" She slung the sauerkraut at Tina, and it landed with a slopping sound on her shoulder.

"Wendy! Winston! Stop it," she heard Elizabeth shout. "Stop it right now."

But the war of the condiments was on. And Wendy was having way too much fun to stop. She flung another handful of sauerkraut in Tina's direction. But Tina ducked, and the sauerkraut hit Elizabeth instead.

The sauerkraut was quickly followed by more mustard and a stream of relish tossed by Hunter. Elizabeth let out an angry shout. "Stop it! Stop it right—"

A shrill whistle brought her up short. Her and everybody else.

Wendy froze, her hand hovering over a mayonnaise bucket.

Ryan, Jessica, Captain Feehan, and the original Hot Dog Howie, owner of Sweet Valley Shore's largest hot-dog franchise, stood there with their hands on their hips.

No one said a word or made a sound.

Ryan stared stone-faced at the mess, then turned an accusing look in Wendy's direction. Just a few hours on the job and already she was in the doghouse!

Chapter
Fifteen

Elizabeth stepped out from beneath the outdoor shower beside the lifeguard station. A heavy hand descended on her shoulder. "Okay. Let's talk."

Ryan spun her around to face him. He looked so forbidding, she fought the urge to cower. "Wendy's a good lifeguard," he said. "But she's got a chronic humor problem. I expected you to keep things in line today. You let me down."

"What was I supposed to do?" Elizabeth cried. "Single-handedly break up a free-for-all?"

Ryan lifted his sunglasses and fixed her with a patient stare. "No. Of course not. No one person could be expected to control those people. But what *should* I expect you to do in a situation like that?"

Elizabeth felt the familiar sinking feeling. Why did she keep falling into this trap with Ryan? Why did she jump on the defensive and let it confuse her logic and reasoning? Why did she keep winding up on the wrong side of every argument?

"Well? If there's trouble, what are you supposed to do? We covered this at least twice during training."

"Flag you," Elizabeth answered in a low tone.

"That's right. Flag me. Flag Captain Feehan. Flag whoever's on duty with you. But call for help *before* things get out of hand. I should have heard your whistle at the first sign of trouble."

"But they were lifeguards," Elizabeth said lamely. "And Winston is my friend. It didn't seem that serious, and then—"

Ryan cut her off abruptly. "It's serious to Hot Dog Howie. Those hot-dog carts are his business. And as far as the rest of it . . . I'm not in charge of Rachel or South Beach. Okay? I don't care if Rachel is a lifeguard. I don't care who any of those people are. You see anybody causing trouble on *this* beach, you blow the whistle."

They stared at each other. Finally Elizabeth spoke. "Am I fired?"

"No. I spoke to Captain Feehan. You and Wendy both get a second chance. Everybody does. It's logistically impossible to fire this many lifeguards at once. Wendy's still at Hot Dog Howie's getting a list of the damages. Everybody involved will have to chip in to cover the cost. Captain Feehan will follow that up with you. You're lucky you're getting a second chance," he said. "Don't blow it."

Ryan turned and walked toward Marcus and Kerry, who were coming back to the station as their shift came to an end.

Nina came out of the lifeguard station and wordlessly handed Elizabeth a towel. Elizabeth angrily rubbed her head and her ponytail. "I don't know how long I can stand this," she sputtered angrily. "Have you ever heard anybody as arrogant and unfair in your life?"

Nina said nothing and shrugged.

Elizabeth stopped toweling and gaped at her friend. "Is that all you're going to do? Shrug?"

"What do you want me to do?"

"I want you to agree with me! I want you to back me up. Why do you keep letting him chew me out like that?"

Nina threw out her hands. "What can I say? He's right. You should have called for help. Beach vendors are an important part of the economy here. We're not police, but we're supposed to keep an eye out for trouble and do what we can."

Elizabeth jutted her jaw. "Nina. We need to talk."

Nina fingered the silver whistle around her neck and dropped her eyes.

"I know you're an old hand around here . . . that you know the ropes. And I know you're Ryan's assistant. But you're also my friend. If you keep patronizing me and throwing your weight around, we're going to have a real problem."

Nina's lashes fluttered up and her dark eyes flashed. "No, Elizabeth. You've got the problem. And the problem is that you're overreacting to everything. You're not thinking about what you're doing and why you're doing it."

"Why are you so against me?" Elizabeth shouted.

"I'm not! I just don't know how to respond to you when you act this way. You're usually hard on yourself. Twenty-four hours a day. You don't *need* anybody riding you. But you're goofing up right and left here. You're making stupid mistakes. And you're not stupid. So why is this happening? And why are you putting me in this squeeze?"

Elizabeth's heart was beating rapidly and there was a lump in her throat. Why *was* she making so many stupid mistakes? Why was she so off balance? Why wasn't her brain working as efficiently as it usually did?

Ryan reappeared in the doorway of the lifeguard station, and Elizabeth caught her breath. Against the dark interior of the station his silhouette looked like a well-muscled Greek statue. The dark glasses were gone.

He stepped out and his face softened. The brown eyes crinkled in reluctant amusement when he looked at Elizabeth. "You know, you were pretty cute with that ketchup streak in your hair."

His gaze held hers for several seconds, and finally she returned his smile, unable to resist the rare moment of warmth. A rush of joy flowed through her and was immediately followed with pangs of guilt and embarrassment.

She knew now why she was goofing up right and left.

And she didn't like the reason.

"So," Ben said, dropping his buoy on the table where Jessica sat. "Here we are."

Jessica handed him the checkout sheet and he made an *X* next to his name, indicating that he had returned his buoy. He was the last one to bring in his equipment. They were alone in the lifeguard station. She could hear Ryan and Nina talking outside.

"Aren't you going to congratulate me for getting on the squad?" he asked.

Jessica studied his face, mentally dissecting the conversation and looking for the needle. Satisfied that there wasn't one, she smiled. "Congratulations."

"Glad I made it?" He smiled and waggled his eyebrows.

"Don't push it," Jessica advised. She wasn't really irritated, though. She was in too good a mood. In fact, she was in such a good mood, she wasn't mad at Ben anymore. And to her surprise, she realized she *was* glad he was on the squad.

Ben sat on the edge of the table and ran a hand over his close-cropped dark hair.

Jessica couldn't help noticing the ripple of

muscle along his arm. He caught her glance and smiled knowingly.

She blushed to the roots of her hair.

"I think we've all built up some muscle tone over the last few days," he said. He reached over and ran the back of his hand along the top of her arm. "You're getting some definition there."

His touch was warm. She looked down at his hand but didn't pull away. Instead she felt her blue-green eyes drawn to his. Ben's blue eyes stared into hers and held her gaze. Unable to look away, she felt herself leaning forward, as if she were being pulled toward him by some invisible force. Her breathing turned shallow when he leaned closer. Jessica actually felt breathless and a little faint. Sure that he was going to kiss her, and eager to feel his lips on hers.

There was a squeak as the door opened.

Ben reared back, and Jessica almost toppled out of her chair. Ryan walked in with Nina behind him and threw a set of keys on the table.

"That's it for the day." He leaned over Jessica's shoulder. "Has everybody turned in their equipment?"

"Yes." Jessica's voice came out hoarse. "I mean, yes," she said in a more composed tone.

Ryan smiled and touched her nose with his index finger. "If you don't have a good sunblock, get one. You've gotten a lot of color today. Your face is bright red."

Jessica felt her face turning even redder as Ben hopped off the table and let out a choking laugh.

Winston examined his reflection in the mirror of the downstairs bathroom he shared with Ben. Mustard. Ketchup. Relish. Sauerkraut. Onions. His tongue snaked out and tasted the unidentifiable concoction on his cheek. Hmmm? Chili, maybe?

His T-shirt and trunks were badly splattered, so he just stepped into the shower fully dressed and turned on the spray. Then he turned his face up toward the nozzle.

Being a clown and a wit could take you a lot of places in life, but it couldn't get him on the Sweet Valley Shore Lifeguard Squad. He hadn't felt like this much of a dweeb since he was in middle school. Winston let out a long, shuddering groan that bounced off the walls of the shower stall and echoed eerily.

Everybody else was at the beach doing important things. Saving lives. Enforcing rules. Getting tan. Picking up dog doo.

What was he doing?

Standing in the shower and washing off the remains of Hot Dog Howie's condiment tray.

"What am I going to do?" he asked himself, his voice barely audible over the groaning pipes. He had enough money from his first tour of star homes to get through the next couple of weeks. But he couldn't stay here all summer without paying his share of rent, phone, and food. And he *had* to be able to call Denise at least once a week.

Full-time unemployment was simply not an option.

He let out a few more moans and groans, and when he was sure he was condiment free, he twisted the knobs and turned off the shower. Dripping wet, he stepped out, pulled his towel off the rack, and began to pat himself dry. He pulled off his wet T-shirt and hung it over the shower. The nylon trunks would dry on their own in a matter of minutes.

The sound of running water continued to circulate through the pipes behind the walls.

He checked to make sure he hadn't left the shower running. He hadn't. Then he looked at the toilet. The water was churning in the bowl.

Winston lifted the cover off the tank on the back and squinted at the apparatus. Hmm. Maybe saving lives wasn't the only manly skill in demand at Sweet Valley Shore. He'd done a little plumbing in his time. If he got right to work on this, he could fix the toilet by dinnertime and probably save the planet thirty gallons of precious water.

Buoyed by a sense of purpose, Winston left the bathroom and marched toward the kitchen, where he knew there was a tool kit under the sink.

In the kitchen Paloma Perro wagged his tail, glad for the company.

"You and me both, pal," Winston said, rummaging under the sink until he found a wrench.

The phone rang. His heart lifted. Maybe it was Denise. He sure hoped so. A sympathetic ear and a few soothing words would be very welcome right now.

He flung himself out of the kitchen, practically dove over the sofa, and lifted the receiver in the middle of the second ring. "Hello?"

"Hello?" a smooth, deep voice said. "May I speak to Wendy?"

"Wendy's not here right now," Winston answered. "Is this Pedro?"

There was a pause. "Is this the guy with the propeller beanie?"

"Well, I'm not actually wearing it at the moment, but yes, this is Winston. May I take a message for Wendy?" he asked in his pleasantest tone.

"Yeah. Tell her I'll pick her up at six o'clock and we'll go out for coffee."

Winston sighed deeply and tapped the phone.

"Well?"

"I'm sorry," Winston said. "But that's no good."

"Okay. Seven, then?"

"What I mean is, that's not a date."

"Sure it's a date."

"Nope. It's not a dream date."

"Who said anything about a dream date?"

"Perhaps I didn't make myself perfectly clear," Winston said calmly. "Wendy happens to be a huge

184

admirer of yours. Taking a girl to a coffee bar, pouring a little caffeine down her throat, and then bringing her home is not the dating behavior of a heartthrob."

There was a long pause at the other end of the line. Then, "I don't think we're on the same wavelength. Maybe we should just forget the whole thing."

"You're right. Maybe we should. So I'll see you bright and early tomorrow morning," Winston said cheerfully. "Hey! I've got an idea. How about I pick up coffee on the way. I'll leave it on your front step. The tourists can watch you drink it while you read the paper."

"I should call the police," Pedro said gloomily.

Winston blanched. Maybe he'd pushed too hard. If Pedro Paloma called the police, he'd find out that Winston had already been forbidden to conduct further tours. And then he wouldn't give Wendy the time of day.

"Oh, what the heck," Pedro said suddenly. "Tell me what you want."

"It's not what I want. It's what Wendy wants. You're the big heartthrob. You know how to make a woman happy. You think of something."

"Look, Winston. I'm just a singer. The heartthrob thing is a myth. An act. A PR thing. I don't know any more about what women want than most guys. The chick is your friend, so you tell me."

185

"Dinner and dancing is always safe," Winston said, feeling like a Little League coach advising a timid young shortstop.

"Dinner and dancing. Isn't that kind of old-fashioned?"

"Maybe. But I've never heard Wendy express an interest in bungee jumping."

"Hmm. Good point. Okay. It's corny. But if that's what she wants, that's what she gets. Tell her I'll pick her up at six. We'll start with a drink at the Boardwalk Café. Have dinner at the Conch. And then go dancing at the Harbor Club."

Winston grinned. "Good plan. I'll give her the message."

"And you and your tour group won't be back?"

"I think I can honestly say you never have to worry about that again."

"Okay. Bye. And stay out of my yard." Pedro hung up the phone with an abrupt click.

Winston hung up the phone, pounded his chest, and let out a Tarzan-style yodel. "You Pedro. Me Matchmaker. Now me fix toilet."

"I can't believe it," Wendy cried. "I'm going to miss the bonfire and cookout!"

"I'm *sorry*," Winston said. "I didn't know about the bonfire and cookout. I'm not a beach employee," he said bitterly. "Remember?"

"*I'm* sorry," she said softly, seeing the real pain in his face. "I know things aren't going your way.

But we're all behind you. We'll help you figure something out."

"Hey! I shouldn't be bumming you out just because *I'm* down in the dumps. You've got a date with a star. I'm sorry I didn't know you had other plans. I shouldn't have accepted for you. That was really out of line. It's not like I'm your social secretary." Wendy kissed him on the cheek. "I'm delighted to have you as my social secretary—now that I'm finally having a social life. I'm also happy to have you stick up for me—even though it did mean I had to spend all afternoon in Hot Dog Howie's office listening to how expensive mustard is."

Winston giggled. "Did you get in trouble?"

"Trouble? I almost got fired." She grinned. "It was worth it, though. I loved seeing Kyle with a face full of mustard." Wendy winked at Winston so he'd know she wasn't really angry and let out a high-pitched, mischievous giggle—like a cartoon chipmunk.

Winston looked relieved. "Want me to call Mr. Paloma and inform him that you're unavailable this evening?" He reached for the phone.

Wendy jumped over the back of the sofa and blocked the path to the phone with her body. "No! If Pedro Paloma wants to go out with me tonight, I'm going. If I cancel, he might not ask me out again." Her heart hammered, and she had a hard time believing he'd really called. "Did he ask anything about me when he called?"

"No," Winston said faintly. "He just, you know, said he was free this evening and wanted to see you."

"He wants to see me," Wendy repeated giddily. She headed for the kitchen. "This is so incredible. I need a cup of tea. And I want to say hello to my Paloma Perro." She put her lips together and whistled.

Paloma Perro came out from beneath the kitchen table with a joyous bark and jumped up, covering her face with wet kisses. "I'm going out with your namesake," she said in baby talk. "Yes, I am. Even if I do have to miss the hottest party of the season so far. It'll be worth it to have the hottest date of my life—so far."

Winston followed her. "Don't be silly. He'll give you a rain check. Go to the bonfire and cookout. It'll be fun."

Wendy gave Paloma Perro a last pat and gently pushed him back down. She opened the refrigerator, removed a soda, and popped the tab. "Nope. You're sweet to try to build up my confidence and all that, but let's be realistic. How often does lightning like Pedro Paloma strike in the same place?"

She laughed, but Winston just looked uncomfortable.

"Hey!" She nudged him on the arm with the cold soda. "That was a joke. Don't get bent."

"I just don't like it when you sell yourself so short."

"Look who's talking," Wendy argued. "If anybody sells himself short, it's you. I think *you* should go to the cookout. You may not be a beach employee, but you'll know everyone there. And if you don't go, it won't be as much fun."

"For who? You're not going to be there."

Wendy pushed her straight hair behind her ear, deliberating. Pedro Paloma might be the most gorgeous man in the state of California, but Winston was her pal. Her buddy. It was Winston who had stood up for her against the South Beach Squad.

"You're absolutely right about Pedro," she said, switching gears. "I'm sure he'll give me a rain check. I'll reschedule with Pedro and go with you so you won't feel uncomfortable."

"Forget it," Winston said, now taking the other side. "If going out with Pedro tonight is what you want, then that's what you should do."

"Hey, guys. What's up?" Ben asked, walking into the kitchen.

The front door banged, and voices floated toward the kitchen from the front hall.

"We were talking about the bonfire," Wendy said.

Ben laughed and jokingly punched Winston's arm. "Heard about your big feud with South Beach. Think they'll try to duke it out with you tonight?"

"No. Because I'm not going," Winston answered.

"Hey! I'm kidding. No way will those guys do anything. Even if they tried, we'd all be there."

"I'm not staying home because of South Beach. I'm staying home because I'm not on the squad. It sort of sounds like a *heroes only* affair."

"Don't be silly," Ben said. "You should definitely go. By the way, who fixed the downstairs toilet?"

"Me," Winston answered.

Ben grinned and lifted his soda in a salute. "That makes you a hero to me."

"You fixed the toilet?" Wendy exclaimed.

Winston waggled the large wrench in his hand. "Yeah. What did you think I was doing with this?"

"Doing with what?"

Suddenly the kitchen seemed awfully crowded as Jessica, Elizabeth, and Nina came through the door in search of refreshments.

"Winston fixed the toilet," Wendy announced. She grinned and pantomimed with her eyebrows and shoulders that they should all make a big fuss.

The whole group burst into wild cheers and applause.

Winston blushed. "Okay, okay. Let's not get silly about this."

"We're trying to talk Winston into going to the cookout and bonfire," Ben said. "He thinks he's not invited."

"Of course you're invited," Nina said briskly.

Winston opened the cabinet under the sink and threw the wrench back in the tool kit. "I don't want to go."

"Why not?" Elizabeth cried.

"I'd feel awkward. Out of place."

"If you feel awkward, just say you're Wendy's date."

"Wendy's already got a date," Winston answered.

The surprised pause was extremely unflattering. Wendy cocked her head at the group and scowled. "Well, thanks a bunch."

Immediately everybody began talking at once, trying to cover up their shock. But Wendy wasn't fooled. She was the last person in the house that anybody expected to have a date. That was crystal clear.

"Who are you going out with?" Nina asked.

"Pedro Paloma," Wendy said nonchalantly.

This time the silence was so deep, Wendy wished somebody would drop a pin just to break the tension.

"You're kidding. How did that happen?" Jessica asked.

"Jessica!" Elizabeth said sharply.

Wendy couldn't help laughing, and she choked on her soda.

"Never mind that," Nina interrupted. "What are you going to wear?"

Chapter Sixteen

"Here's a good one," Nina shouted. She lifted the large dry stick of driftwood and waved it triumphantly at Paul.

Paul came sliding down the dune on the sides of his sandals with an armload of driftwood he had gathered. "Put it on top," he instructed.

Nina placed the stick on top of the bundle in his arms. Paul had been the first person she'd seen when she arrived at the South Beach tower where the bonfire was being held.

He'd immediately grabbed her arm and insisted they consider this their first date. "That means you can only dance with me," he teased, reminding her of the promise she had extracted from him at the Sand Bar.

Paul sure was different from Bryan—in every way. Bryan rarely flirted, never danced, and hardly paid any attention at all to his clothes.

Paul looked as if he'd stepped out of a menswear

catalog. He wore pressed khaki shorts and a red T-shirt with a canvas windbreaker. His light brown skin was absolutely flawless. Nina couldn't help wondering if his cheek was as smooth as it looked, and what it would feel like to rub her face against his.

"Let's take this load back to the bonfire, and then I'll take you to my own private driftwood source. But you have to promise to keep it a secret."

"I'm pretty good at keeping secrets," Nina said.

"Are you good at keeping secrets from Bryan?" he teased.

"I told you . . ."

"I know. You told me you have a serious boyfriend. That's great because I'm a very unserious guy. So I could be your unserious boyfriend."

"One boyfriend is plenty for me," she said sternly as they approached the group that had gathered for the party.

The big crowd included the employees of Sweet Valley Shore, South Beach, the Port Halley Squad, the North Sound Squad, and the Four Mile Beach Squad.

In all there were probably about two hundred people laughing and talking and dancing to the rock and roll blasting through a boom box.

Rachel was there in a tight white denim miniskirt and a black cotton halter top. Her long dark hair hung loose and blew provocatively in the early evening breeze. Several good-looking guys stood around her, laughing and trying to engage her in conversation.

Nina noted with amusement that the other big female draw was Jessica. Even two guys from the South Beach Squad seemed to have joined her court. Hunter, the good-looking guy with red curls. And one of the new people on the South Beach Squad. A tall guy with a blond ponytail.

"Have you seen Ryan?" Nina asked as Paul dumped the load of driftwood on top of the growing pile.

Paul shook his head.

Nina thoughtfully watched Jessica's growing circle of admirers. Some guys worked harder when they thought they had a little competition. Would Ryan?

Paul took her elbow, temporarily distracting her from her matchmaking schemes. "Come on. I'll show you where I get all my driftwood. My secret source of supply. As a matter of fact, I collect driftwood."

"You collect driftwood?"

He took her hand. "You said you were good at keeping secrets. So I'm trusting you with my biggest secret. I'm a geek. In fact, I'm so geeky that my hobby is whittling."

"Whittling's not geeky," she protested. "It's very masculine."

"It is? I thought girls would think of whittling as sort of a old-man-on-the-front-porch thing."

"No," she responded with a giggle. "I think of it as a hunting-and-gathering-survival-of-the-manliest thing."

"Really?" He stood up straighter and looked

194

pleased. Then he became comically furtive, narrowing his eyes and looking around. "Don't tell anybody anyway. I don't want them horning in on my supply."

The sun was setting, and it hung like a fluorescent orange ball of flame over the choppy water. White horizontal lines rippled offshore, moving at an angle with the rising wind.

The evening was cool, and Nina wished she had worn something a little heavier than her white cotton camp shirt and blue-and-white-striped cotton pajama-style pants.

She shivered, and Paul released her hand. "Here." He removed his windbreaker and draped it over her shoulders.

"Thanks." She smiled.

"This way." He took her hand again and pulled her toward a high dune.

Nina hung back slightly, feeling suddenly wary. They had wandered a fairly good distance from the party. It was getting dark. And Paul was coming on awfully strong.

"Come on," he urged. "While there's still enough light to see."

She swallowed her nervousness. She was being ridiculous. Ridiculous and dishonest. It wasn't Paul she was afraid of. It was herself. Nina was a lot more attracted to him than she wanted to admit. If he were to put his arms around her and continue giving her the smile he was giving her now . . .

"Nina, what's wrong?"

Startled from her reverie, she forced a light laugh. "Sorry. I was just thinking about something else for a minute." She hurried to catch up with him, and as they reached the top of the dune Nina gasped.

On the other side of the dune lay a beautiful stretch of completely pristine beach. The sand was smooth and white and dotted with graceful pieces of driftwood.

"When there's a storm, the tide comes way in and washes a lot of stuff up on this part of the beach. Then when it recedes, this is what's left. There's hardly ever anybody here because it's a long way from the swimming beach and there's no road. So I have it pretty much to myself."

He leaned over and picked up a piece of driftwood. His long, tapered fingers turned it this way and that, examining it in the fading light. "It's a porpoise," he announced.

"Huh?"

He made a sudden move toward her, and she jumped back with a slight shriek.

His face registered mild shock, and then he laughed. "Don't be so nervous. I just wanted to reach into the pocket of my windbreaker. You can do it. Put your hand in the right pocket."

Feeling completely ridiculous, Nina reached into the pocket of the windbreaker. Her hand closed over something smooth and hard. She removed the object and marveled. "You made this?"

"No. The sea made it. All I did was whittle away the

parts that didn't need to be there so you could see it."

Nina held up the beautifully carved miniature figure. "Is it a whale?"

"No. It's a manatee. They're almost extinct. Most people think they're ugly, but for some reason I'm really into them." He straightened it in the palm of her hand. "I like carving. When I get a bunch of them done, maybe I'll sell them on the boardwalk. Send the money to the Save the Manatee Fund or something."

"You're very talented," she commented. "If you're an artist, you should go to art school."

"Nah. Whittling is just something I do for fun. It's just a craft. I'm not really interested in art."

"But you're interested in manatees. And saving them. Marine biology is a great field. And there are a lot of good schools here in California. Why don't you pursue that as a career?"

Paul closed her fingers over the little statue. "Lifeguard. Student. Career counselor. You're a busy girl, Nina Harper."

The last bit of the sun was fading, and Paul returned her interested gaze. Then he leaned closer, his lips curving. Automatically she lifted her face.

He placed a light kiss on her lips, then drew back his head and put a finger to her mouth. "Another secret to keep."

Jessica smiled stiffly at the blond guy with the ponytail. His name was Peter. He was on the

South Beach Squad. And he'd tried to come on to her the other night in the Sand Bar. He didn't seem to be able to take a hint. Or a hike. Every time she tried to break away and talk to somebody else, he followed her.

"So, Jessica, who do you like to dance to? I'll ask Barney to put it on the CD player."

"That's okay," Jessica replied. "Don't bother. I'm not really in the mood for dancing." She hoped she sounded firm. "Excuse me, I'm going to get something to drink."

She wore a blue cotton rib-knit sweater and a tight pair of jeans. It was a different look for her. Sexy, but casual. It was really more Elizabeth's style than hers, but she thought maybe it would make her seem more serious and appeal to Ryan. Where was he, anyway?

"I'll come with you," Peter offered.

Jessica gritted her teeth and took a deep breath. Would it be considered a faux pas if she told a fellow lifeguard to buzz off?

"What can I get you?" Peter asked eagerly when they reached the metal tubs full of soda cans.

"I'll get it myself," she said, reaching into the ice.

Somebody changed the music, and Peter's shoulders twitched to the beat. "This is more like it. Feel like dancing now?"

"I told you . . ."

Ben suddenly appeared at her side, wrapping a possessive arm around her waist as he gave her a kiss.

"Hi, hon! Sorry to take so long with the fire." He removed the soda from her hand, took a deep gulp, and handed it back to her. "So what's going on?" He lifted his brows and gave Peter an inquisitive smile.

Peter's mouth opened slightly in surprise. Ben was coming off like a real steady boyfriend who, in the friendliest way possible, was telling another guy to back off.

"We were just talking about music," Peter said, taking a step back and changing gears.

"I'm Ben. Sweet Valley Shore Squad." Ben extended his hand.

"Peter. South Beach Squad. So you two are working together?"

"Yeah. We're really happy we both made the Sweet Valley squad. And since we live together, it works out really well."

Jessica put her soda can to her mouth to hide her smile. Peter took another step backward. "I see. Well, then, uh, you guys take it easy and I'll see you around." Peter wandered away, and within seconds he attached himself to another curvaceous blonde.

"Wow! What a fickle guy," Ben commented.

Jessica laughed. "Thanks for rescuing me. You were very convincing."

"Why shouldn't I be? I learned the imaginary boyfriend routine from an expert."

Jessica moved out of his embrace. "Ha, ha!" she said dryly.

"I'm not ragging on you," he insisted in a

friendly voice. "I'm just teasing. Like a friend. Can't we be friends, Jessica? We're housemates. We're squad mates. It would be nice if we could get along."

"Well," Jessica mused. "Maybe. As long as we're clear on the *just friends* part."

"Just friends," Ben confirmed. "Unless you conclude that Ryan Taylor is the impossible dream and decide to settle for a mere mortal."

All Jessica's friendly feelings toward Ben evaporated. "You know, I have a hard time believing you're a genius. Because if you're trying to get on my good side, it seems like you'd know enough to quit insulting me."

"Who's insulting you?"

"You are. Why would Ryan turn out to be an impossible dream? What's so far-fetched about him being interested in me?"

Ben opened his mouth and popped his jaw, like somebody who was dying to say something but was restraining himself.

"Come on. Let it all out. You've been completely insulting so far. Why turn tactful now?"

"Okay. I just don't think Ryan is your type. And vice versa. I know Nina wants you two to get together. But Ryan seems like . . . I don't know . . . somebody with really high standards."

Jessica's eyes bulged. "What?"

"Wait, wait. Wait! That didn't come out right."

Jessica began stalking away. It was time to

have a talk with Nina. She didn't want Nina discussing her or her love life with Ben.

He caught at the sleeve of her cotton sweater. "Listen to me. What I meant is he's a guy with *impossible* standards. Nina said he has himself down for every single shift. Every day he gets up at six A.M. and runs ten miles. He pushes himself to the absolute limit. There's no middle ground for guys like that. They set impossible standards for themselves—and for everybody else, too. Do you really think somebody that intense is going to make you happy?"

"Aren't you intense?"

"Yes. But in a different way. I don't expect everybody to be like me. In fact, I'm a lot happier when they're not. I don't have unrealistic expectations that can't be met."

Jessica pulled her arm away from him. "You may be in Mensa," she said. "But as far as I'm concerned, you're a fool. You think I can't meet *Ryan's* standards. In case you haven't noticed, Ryan hasn't criticized me. *You* have. Ryan doesn't make fun of my clothes and my makeup. *You* do. Ryan doesn't tear me down. So who's got the standards I can't meet? Hmm?"

Jessica stalked off, so angry and upset that her hands were shaking.

"Jessica!" she heard Ben call out.

But she ignored him and kept going. The sharp smell of kerosene filled the air and was followed by a snap and a crackle. A cheer went up as the bonfire sprang to life.

That was when Jessica saw Rachel watching her. Watching her and Ben—backlit by the flames, and glaring like a she-devil.

"Your dog is named Paloma?" Pedro sat back in his chair and laughed. "I don't know whether I'm incredibly flattered or totally insulted."

Wendy wiped delicately at the edge of her mouth with her napkin. "Oh, it's a compliment. Definitely. Naming livestock after people we admire is an old family tradition."

"Has anybody ever told you you're funny?"

"Everybody tells me I'm funny," she said truthfully.

He leaned forward and lifted her hand from the table. "Has anybody ever told you you're beautiful?"

"Never."

"You are," he said. His large brown eyes met hers and his dark brows arched in a way that seemed to indicate that he had just discovered the fact himself.

Sitting here in Jessica's white linen slacks and Nina's silver silk tank that was almost the exact same color as her eyes, Wendy felt glamorous and beautiful.

Maybe it wasn't the clothes that made her feel that way. Maybe it was the Boardwalk Café. The outdoor bar featured small, intimate tables for two. On every table a votive candle flickered in a frosted glass container tall enough to protect the flame from the ocean breeze.

Maybe it wasn't her clothes *or* the setting that made her feel desirable. Maybe it was Pedro.

Wendy searched his face for the crack in his sincerity. The dialogue was right out of some sappy second-rate romance movie. Handsome Latino woos plain American girl in an effort to con her. Plain American girl is so pathetically grateful for attention, she falls for it hook, line, and sinker.

"What are you thinking?" he asked suddenly.

Wendy blushed guiltily. "Why do you ask?" she countered. Answering a question with a question was a time-honored, tried-and-true method of avoiding telling the truth.

"Because you suddenly looked . . . I don't know . . . suspicious."

She jumped slightly. Had he been reading her mind? Her eyes narrowed again. Or was there some reason she *should* be suspicious?

This time *his* face colored slightly and he looked troubled. In an instant the look was gone and his handsome features had settled back into a serene, relaxed expression. "Let's move on. The night's young and I made dinner reservations at the Conch."

He reached into the pocket of his black jeans, removed some money, and left a few bills on the table. Then he politely held the back of her chair while she got up and removed her cardigan from the back of the chair. Gracefully and gallantly he draped it around her shoulders.

She could feel the stares as they left the romantic outdoor café. Her eyes met those of a girl slightly younger than herself. The girl was staring at Wendy as if she were studying every detail of Wendy's dress and demeanor.

Wendy glanced away and realized that a second woman was staring at her. Embarrassed to be caught staring, the woman turned her attention to her own companion and began an animated conversation.

Wendy swiveled her head and realized that lots of women were looking at her. But not because she was pretty or well dressed. Because she was with Pedro Paloma, who, even if they'd never heard of the singing sensation, was easily the handsomest man in the place.

Wendy felt thrilled, insulted, and gratified all at once. "Do you ever get used to people looking at you?" she asked softly as they strolled along the boardwalk in the direction of the restaurant.

"It can be embarrassing, but after a while you just learn to filter it out. If it's bothering you, we can go someplace less public."

"It's not bothering me exactly. It's just a new experience. Having people look at me, I mean. I'm sort of the invisible type. Or at least I have been until tonight."

He brushed her hair back off her shoulders and lifted her chin with his fingertips. "Nobody should feel invisible. Ever. I have an old family tradition. When someone feels invisible, we have a cure."

Pedro said something softly in Spanish. Then he lifted her face and tenderly kissed her on the lips.

When he drew back his head, she felt slightly dizzy, breathless, and embarrassed. "That's quite a custom," she said.

"Yes. I think it probably beats naming the livestock. But now, Wendy, the curse of invisibility is gone. And you will shine like a beautiful star forever."

"Wow!" she breathed. "That's so beautiful. When did that custom start?"

He grimaced. "I was afraid you were going to ask me that. The truth is, I just made it up. It seemed like a perfect way to get you to kiss me."

She widened her eyes. "Really?"

He laughed. "Really? I'm a kissing bandit. And I'm also hungry." He took her hand and tugged. "Let's go to dinner."

Heads continued to swivel as they passed. Wendy smiled to herself. Pedro might have made it up, but it seemed to be working. She didn't feel invisible. And as shallow as it seemed, the only thing she wished was that everybody she knew wasn't at the bonfire and cookout.

She'd sure love to sashay past a table of South Beach lifeguards on Pedro Paloma's arm—and act like *they* were invisible.

Chapter
Seventeen

"Glad you came?" Elizabeth asked.

Winston nodded and took a bite of his hot dog. "Yeah. I've met some really cool people and I've actually gotten a few job leads."

Elizabeth chewed on the edge of a taco chip. She wished she had an appetite, but she didn't. She felt ill at ease and unsettled.

Even though she'd made the squad, the afternoon had been a disaster. There was an awkward tension between her and Nina. And Elizabeth was feeling awkward around her sister. Jessica had made her interest in Ryan obvious. And it was looking more and more like Ryan returned that interest. Elizabeth knew she should be happy for Jessica. But picturing Jessica and Ryan together was making her miserable—and she hated herself for feeling that way.

"You don't look like you're having a good time," Winston commented.

"I guess I'm really not," Elizabeth said, dropping the rest of the taco chip into a big garbage Dumpster.

"Missing Tom?"

Elizabeth nodded, guiltily realizing she hadn't thought about Tom in the last two hours.

"I'm sure missing Denise. Funny thing. When she's gone, I feel the loneliest when I'm in a big crowd like this."

"Me too. I suppose it's because everybody else seems to be so happy and part of a couple. And we're feeling so lonely and conspicuously single."

"Who's lonely?"

Ben materialized out of the dark beside Winston, and Elizabeth felt a little stab of irritation. She didn't know him very well, but Ben was turning out to be rather ubiquitous. "Do you work for the CIA or something?" she snapped. "It seems like you're always materializing out of nowhere."

Her voice sounded downright nasty, and Winston gave her a look that was almost as surprised and hurt as the one Ben gave her.

"Don't *you* start on me," Ben pleaded. "I've gotten enough flack from your sister."

"I'm sorry," Elizabeth apologized.

"If I'm butting in too much, I'm sorry. I'm just trying to fit in with everybody. But I'm obviously going about it the wrong way."

"No, you're not," Winston argued. "And we owe you an apology. Most of us have known each other a long time, and we probably haven't made as much effort to be friends as we should have."

Elizabeth felt ashamed of herself. Ben *was* eager to be friends. And he *was* the odd man out. They'd all been so wrapped up in their own concerns, they hadn't been as receptive to a new friendship as they should have been.

And Jessica had been horrible.

Then again, Ben had a rather abrasive personality. And he had deliberately rubbed Jessica the wrong way more than once.

Winston draped an arm around Ben's shoulders. "C'mon, Ben, let's bond—talk about some guy stuff and get to know each other."

"I don't have time to bond," Ben answered with a grin. "Captain Feehan asked me to go to the lifeguard station and get another can of kerosene."

"Elizabeth will get it," Winston said airily. "Won't you?"

"I don't know," she said. "I might bother Ryan."

Ben lifted his baseball cap and scratched his head. "According to Captain Feehan, Ryan drove to Port Halley for the evening. Captain Feehan gave me the keys to the station." He held them up and jingled them.

Winston drew Ben closer. "See?" he told Elizabeth. "No need to be concerned. You won't bother anybody." He waved his hand. "Now off with you. We have masculine things to do. We're going to beat drums and chant and get in touch with our feminine sides." He turned to Ben. "Tell me, Ben. Do you shave? Or wax?"

Ben looked confused and a little nervous. "Wax what?"

"I'm out of here." Elizabeth laughed. "Tell Captain Feehan I'll be back in a little while with the kerosene." As she walked away she heard Winston regaling Ben with stories about his life in an all-female dorm.

Well, at least Winston and Ben were having a good time, Elizabeth reflected. But she wasn't. After she returned with the kerosene, she'd stay a few more minutes to be polite, then she'd go home and try reaching Tom again.

An imperious finger tapped Jessica on the shoulder. She turned and saw Rachel's malevolent eyes staring at hers. "Didn't I tell you to leave Ben alone?"

"Hey! I have no interest in Ben. Okay? And I really don't understand why you do. But if you don't leave me alone, I'm going to—"

"Going to what? Tell on me?" Rachel smiled pleasantly. "Listen, Jessica. I'm not a nice person."

"Neither is Ben. So I guess you two are perfect for each other."

"That's what I think. And that's what Ben *used* to think. But Ben is a very aggressive and persistent guy. If he thinks he wants you, he's going to keep chasing until he gets what he wants. So my advice to you is keep running from him unless you want to run from me."

Jessica lifted her lip in a sneer. "You don't scare me, Rachel. But you do bore me. So I'm out of here. And my advice to *you* is—quit bugging me."

She furiously pushed past Rachel. It was bad enough having Ben all over her. Having Rachel nipping at her heels every time she turned around was more than she could stand.

This was the weirdest triangle she'd ever been a part of. And she wanted out.

She didn't want to fight with Rachel.

She didn't want to deal with Ben.

She just wanted them both out of her hair.

If Rachel was that interested in Ben, then she'd probably back off when and if she was convinced that Jessica's romantic interests lay elsewhere.

She cut through the crowd that was dancing to old sixties surfing tunes. Nina was dancing with Paul and tried to wave her over. "Come dance with us," she called out.

Jessica waved back but didn't respond to the invitation. She kept going, quickening her step as she left the party area.

She was going to the lifeguard station. And once she got there, she was going to give Ryan the full Jessica Wakefield treatment. Fling herself on him if she had to. Tie him up and take him back to the party with her.

Jessica wanted Rachel to get it through her

thick skull that she planned to get a guy better than Ben. Way better.

"Then Denise turned to me and . . ." Winston trailed off. He hadn't had Ben's full attention for quite a while.

Ben's lively eyes had been glued to an animated exchange between Jessica and Rachel. Both girls had stalked off in opposite directions. Rachel toward the South Beach Squad, which was boogying next to the large speaker. Jessica in the direction of the house.

"Think Jessica's going home already?" Winston watched as Jessica's blond hair disappeared into the dark as she moved down the beach.

"I hope not. But Rachel is a girl who can kill your party mood."

"What's with you and Rachel?"

"Ugly story," Ben said shortly. "Listen, I need to have a word with Rachel. Then I'm going to call it a night." He shook Winston's hand. "It's going to be a great summer. Plan on having a blast." He clapped Winston's shoulder, then walked off like a man with a distasteful job to do.

Winston watched him approach the tall, gorgeous Rachel and wished he knew what that story was all about. Suddenly he realized he had that lonely-in-the-crowd feeling again.

"I'm going to call Denise," he muttered out loud. He dropped his paper cup into a wastebasket and began walking away toward the house.

If Ben wasn't going to stay, he wasn't either. He'd met some nice people, but he didn't have anybody to dance with. He didn't have anybody to talk to. And he wanted to be home when Wendy got there.

He smiled to himself. The only bright spot in the evening was knowing that he'd played some part in making Wendy's dream date come true.

Elizabeth put the key into the lock and turned it, pushing open the door to the lifeguard station. The overhead light was already on, and the door that led to Ryan's quarters was closed.

She shut the front door and put the key down on the table underneath the window. Above it was a set of cabinets. Maybe a can of kerosene was in there.

She reached up and tugged at the handles. The doors to the cabinets didn't open. They were stuck. She pulled harder, rattling them and making a loud clatter that echoed in the empty station.

"Can I help you find something?"

Elizabeth let out a shriek and whirled around.

Ryan stood in the doorway of his room. Barefooted, he wore a pair of jeans and no shirt. A towel hung from his neck, and the ends of his short brown curls were wet. It was obvious he'd just stepped out of the shower. Beads of water still clung to his darkly tanned shoulders and glistened like jewels.

"I thought you were gone," Elizabeth said. "Captain Feehan said you went to Port Halley."

"I got back a few minutes ago."

There was a long silence. Ryan bent his head and rubbed his hair with the towel. Then he looked up.

His brown eyes met her blue-green ones, and Elizabeth's breath caught in her chest.

The silence deepened, and Elizabeth wondered if he could hear the thundering of her heart.

She knew she should say something. But she didn't. She couldn't.

Ryan walked slowly toward her until they stood inches apart. He lifted his hand, and Elizabeth waited for him to touch her. Instead he reached up over her head and gently pressed the corner of the left-hand cabinet. The catch sprang, and the door swung slowly open. "What was it you wanted?" he asked in a whisper, his head bent over hers.

Unable to stop herself, Elizabeth closed her eyes and lifted her face. Their lips touched, and her arms flew around his neck. His arms encircled her waist and lifted her off her feet, crushing her against his bare chest.

"Elizabeth," he whispered hoarsely before covering her face and neck with kisses so passionate, she felt as if a tidal wave had swept them both away.

Wendy rested her cheek on her hand and sighed. "This is too good to be true. I'm going to wake up in a minute and realize I'm in a dream."

Pedro leaned across the table and pinched her arm.

"Ow!"

"See? You're not dreaming."

"You know, you're nothing like I thought you'd be," she said. "You look like the man of my dreams, but you act a whole lot like one of my brothers. May I have one of those rolls, please?"

He politely passed her the bread basket. "While we're on the subject, you're not what I expected either. When Winston brought this up—"

"Winston! What about Winston?" Wendy abruptly interrupted, her hand frozen over the bread basket.

"Umm. I don't know. Did I say something about Winston?"

"You said something about *when Winston brought this up.* Brought what up? Did Winston talk to you about me?"

Pedro fidgeted slightly in his chair. "Sure," he said. "When I called you to make the date."

"I asked Winston if you said anything about me, and he said no."

Pedro smiled nervously. "I guess he just didn't want you to know that I was, well . . . nervous about taking you out. All I did was ask a few questions about you. You know? Like . . . what kind of food you enjoyed. Stuff like that."

He was lying. Wendy *knew* he was lying, and her

stomach clenched. "You didn't seem nervous when you talked to me at the Sand Bar."

Pedro sat back and leaned his elbow on the arm of his chair, his white teeth chewing nervously at his lower lip. He seemed to be conducting an internal debate. He looked up at her from beneath one quizzical brow. "Exactly how good *is* your sense of humor?"

"Why do you ask?" Wendy asked slowly.

He cleared his throat and sat forward. He gestured with his hands, as if he were bracing her. "First of all, let me say that Winston Egbert did me one of the biggest favors of my life when he asked me to take you out."

"Winston *asked* you to take me out?" she whispered, feeling almost sick with humiliation.

"No. Well, yes. That's not what I mean. What I meant was I didn't *know* Winston was doing me a favor when he asked me to take you out."

"So Winston *did* ask you to take me out? You didn't just look at me in the Sand Bar and say to yourself, 'Boy! There's a girl I'd like to meet.' Winston *asked* you to do it!" She dropped her napkin on the table. "Wow! Pedro, you're a really nice guy. Do you take out girls as a favor to every stranger in a bar? Or did Winston make it worth your while?"

"You're angry."

"You made a fool out of me," she said, her throat tightening.

215

"That wasn't my intention," he said in a soft voice.

Tears clouded Wendy's vision, and the features of Pedro's handsome face blurred. It was as if he were melting. Her beautiful dream was melting. This was worse than waking up and finding out it wasn't true.

"I have to go," she said, standing so quickly that her chair fell over.

The noise attracted the attention of several people seated around them, and there was a momentary pause in the happy and excited chatter of the restaurant.

Wendy grabbed her purse and plunged blindly toward the door. She could hear murmurs and whispers behind her, but she didn't care.

Once she was out on the boardwalk, she began to run.

"Wendy! Wendy, please wait."

She continued to run and felt the boards beneath her quiver as he chased her. Pedro's long legs quickly closed the distance between them. He caught her by the arm and pulled her to a stop so fast that they collided, chest to chest. He steadied her by wrapping his arms tightly around her shoulders.

"Let me go!" she demanded with her face pressed into the neck of his shirt.

"Listen to me. I'll tell you everything. We'll fight about it once. And then we'll never fight about anything ever again."

"Stop it!" she yelled, pushing against his chest.

But Pedro held on tighter. "Winston said he'd take my house off the walking tour if I'd go out with you. I agreed. And I've never been so happy to be blackmailed in my life. I think you're great. You're funny. You're beautiful. And I think I'm falling in love with you."

That did it. Wendy had had all the canned come-on she could take for one night. She broke out of his grasp and swung at him with her purse, landing a blow on his upper arm. "Knock it off, you fraud."

"Ouch!" he protested.

"See! You're not dreaming either," she said through clenched teeth. She swung again and caught him on the other arm. "Exactly how good is my sense of humor? About *this* good." She lifted her purse again. "Let's see how good *your* sense of humor is, Romeo."

Pedro successfully dodged the third blow by jumping back. He held up his hands in surrender. "I'm sorry. Let's call this our first fight and move on to the makeup portion of the evening." He opened his arms. "There's an old custom that—"

Wendy lunged with her purse.

This time he vaulted lightly over the rail of the boardwalk. He landed on the sand below and looked up, as if she were leaning over a balcony. "I guess that means you don't want me to walk you home."

Chapter
Eighteen

Jessica stopped a few yards away from the lifeguard station, bent forward, and shook out her
hair. When she tossed back her head, the blond
mane stood out all around her face, framing it like
a halo.

She wet her lips and loosened her shoulders. It
was important to stay loose when making an all-
out attack on a guy. Important to look him in the
eye, not turn shy and look away.

A flutter of nervous embarrassment stopped
her just outside the door. If it didn't work, Jessica
knew she'd look like a total fool. And she'd have
to live with the failure all summer. Could she continue to work with Ryan if she threw herself at
him and got rejected?

She took a step back. Love had been a rocky
road. Did she want to risk another bump?

"No guts, no glory," she chided herself. Then,

squaring her shoulders again, she pushed open the door.

Somewhere deep in the fog Elizabeth heard a scream. Ryan's arms released her, and he broke away so suddenly, she almost fell.

Dizzy from his kisses, she shook her head and lifted the lids of her eyes.

Jessica stood in the doorway, frozen like a statue. One hand covered her mouth, and her blue-green eyes looked as horrified and embarrassed as Elizabeth felt.

"Jessica," Elizabeth squeaked. Then she went blank. What could she say? Not only had she cruelly betrayed Tom, she had betrayed Jessica, too.

Elizabeth had been sure that Ryan's interest was targeted at Jessica. It was clear to her now that *she* had been the object of Ryan's interest from day one. His rude and unfriendly behavior must have been an attempt to deny his attraction and hide his feelings.

Ryan seemed to recover first. He cleared his throat. "Did you need something, Jessica?" he asked in a kind tone. "Did somebody send you to get me?"

He was offering Jessica a graceful way out of her humiliating situation. Making it seem as if he were unaware that she had come to see him.

But Jessica must have been too unnerved to realize that. She didn't respond in a way that would save herself, him, and Elizabeth a lot of embarrassment.

She cast one last, accusatory look at Elizabeth. Then she backed out of the door.

Elizabeth hurried after her, but Ryan stopped her. "Elizabeth, wait. Please."

She turned, and he dragged his hand down over his face. "I'm sorry. That was totally unprofessional, and it won't happen again."

Elizabeth's heart was still racing, and her knees felt week.

"What I'm trying to say is . . . if anything I said or did made you feel pressured . . ."

"You didn't pressure me and you know it," she managed to say. "So don't apologize."

His lips curved inward and he looked as if he were trying hard to put a set of complex thoughts into carefully chosen words. "You have a boyfriend. And I have a job to do. This has the potential to be a major problem. In fact, it looks like the problems have already begun."

"I agree," she said softly.

"So I think, if we can, we should forget this."

She nodded.

He squeezed his eyes regretfully. "Do I owe Jessica an apology?" he asked. "I know she thought that I . . . that she . . . that she and I . . ."

"I don't know what to say about that," Elizabeth said truthfully. "But I think I'd better go home now and see what I can do."

He took her arm and guided her to the door. "Friends?"

"Friends," she confirmed, working hard to look him in the eye. It wasn't easy. Not after the passionate interlude they had just shared.

He slowly released her arm and stood in the doorway, watching as she left the station and walked down the beach.

It was dark now. Elizabeth could see the flickering lights of their beach house.

She couldn't resist taking one last look over her shoulder. Ryan was still standing in the doorway, bathed in the light that poured out of the open door. Tall. Broad shouldered. Vigilant.

Would she ever forget that kiss? Could she?

Her fingers brushed her swollen lips.

Never.

Choking and sobbing, Jessica broke into a run when she saw the house. All she wanted now was to get to her room, shut the door, and die.

"Jessica!" Ben's deep voice floated toward her from the oleander bushes that grew along the side of the house.

As if things weren't bad enough.

"Jessica, wait!"

Miserably Jessica came to a stop and turned to face him. There was nothing he could do or say to her now that would make things any worse.

The minute he saw her face, his brow furrowed

in concern. "Jess! What's the matter?"

Jessica could only sob furiously.

Ben's face wore a look of dawning understanding. "The Ryan thing went south. Right?"

"Right," Jessica said. "So I guess you're thrilled. You're a genius, Ben. You were one hundred percent correct. If you want to say 'I told you so,' go ahead and sa . . ." She couldn't finish. Her entire body began to shake with fresh sobs. Her head . . . her lips . . . and her shoulders.

"I'm sorry," he said softly. And the next thing she knew, he was holding her in his arms and stroking her hair. "I'm really sorry." His voice was so kind, so sincere, her arms automatically wrapped around his waist. She clung to him, grateful for the comfort.

"I'm an idiot," she wept.

"No, you're not."

"I'm stupid. It wasn't me he wanted. It was Elizabeth."

She felt Ben stiffen.

"Ryan and Elizabeth? I thought Elizabeth had a boyfriend."

"She does," Jessica confirmed, her grief beginning to recede a little. "His name is Tom, and she's supposed to be in love with him. If she's so in love with Tom, why was she kissing Ryan?"

"Well," he said lightly. "There's love. And then there's *love*."

"What does that mean?" she asked irritably.

"It means that sometimes you see somebody and your heart goes boom. But you're responding to things that ultimately don't matter much. Then you realize that you don't love that person at all. In fact, you can't stand them."

Jessica pulled gently out of Ben's embrace and accepted the bandanna he pulled from his back pocket. "Are you talking about Elizabeth or you and Rachel?" She dabbed at her eyes and nose.

"Me and Rachel," he admitted.

"You may not love her, but she thinks she loves you."

He laughed. "She doesn't love me. She just doesn't know how to take no for an answer. Look, about Ryan, it's for the best. Really."

"No, it's not," she said, giving her nose a loud blow as she began to pull herself together.

"What do you mean?" Ben asked.

Jessica closed her eyes and conjured a picture of her sister and Ryan in a passionate embrace. A spark of outrage ignited a fire in her chest. Grief and humiliation hardened into anger and renewed determination.

"I mean, it's not for the best. And it's not over until I say it's over."

"Jessica," Ben warned.

"I don't take no for an answer either," Jessica said grimly to Ben. "And I'm not licked yet." She shoved the bandanna at him and put her hands on her hips. "I'm going to get Ryan Taylor."

Ben threw his arms up in disgust and stomped up the walk. "I was wrong!" he shouted. "Jessica Wakefield, you *are* an idiot." He slammed the door shut, and inside the house Paloma began barking when he heard the noise.

Jessica didn't care what Ben thought. All she cared about now was telling her sneaky, cheating, two-timing sister that Ryan was too good for her.

"Denise! Denise Waters!" Winston shouted into the telephone. At the other end of the line the Italian hotel operator rattled off something rapid and incomprehensible. The only word that sounded vaguely familiar was *palazzo*. Or did she say pizzeria? Maybe she was telling him that Denise had gone out for a pizza.

"Could I leave a message?"

"Como?"

"Messag-o. Tell-*a* her-*a* that-*a* Winston Egbert called," he shouted in a heavy, fake Italian accent.

"Como?"

The door shut with an angry bang that shook the windows in their frames. Ben strode angrily through the living room, his sneakers making a loud squeak on the floor.

"Como?" Winston muttered curiously.

"I still don't see why you're so worried," Paul said with a laugh, pulling his car keys from his pocket and opening the door of his blue Toyota for Nina. "They're all adults."

They were in the South Beach parking lot, and she could hear the party rocking on behind them.

"Just call it a hunch," Nina said. "All of a sudden I realized that none of my housemates were at the party. All I want to do is run back to the house and make sure everybody's cool, and then we'll come back to the bonfire. It'll take five minutes."

He shook his head. "Lifeguard. Career counselor. And housemother, too," he teased. "You *are* busy."

Elizabeth stopped on the walkway outside the house. Inside, she could see Ben walking back and forth from the living room to the kitchen and into the hall. His movements were fast and jerky. The body language was clear. He was angry.

And he wasn't the only one. Jessica stood on the porch with her arms crossed over her chest and her eyes glittering dangerously. "I can't believe you did this to me."

"Jessica. I didn't do anything. Please let me—"

Jessica uncrossed her arms and started down the stairs with her hands balled into fists. "For once I was excelling and you were failing. And you just couldn't stand it." Jessica's voice grew louder and more accusatory. "So you decided to make a fool out of me by going behind my back and stealing Ryan."

"That's not true," Elizabeth protested, her

225

heart sinking. Obviously Jessica was determined to make a scene. Determined to be irrational and unreasonable. But she'd been hurt, and Elizabeth felt sorry for her. Instead of hitting back, she should try to make Jessica feel better.

"You did, too. You knew I liked him and that he liked me. How did you get him to kiss you like that—pretend to be me? And what about Tom?"

That did it. Elizabeth quit feeling sorry for her twin. Jessica had hit too low. And she'd struck a nerve when she'd mentioned Tom. "Leave Tom out of this!" Elizabeth shouted.

"You're supposed to be in love with him," Jessica bellowed.

"Quit shouting at me," Elizabeth bellowed back.

"Quit stealing my boyfriends just because your own won't return your phone calls!" Jessica screamed.

"Ryan's not your boyfriend," Elizabeth screamed back, feeling furious with Jessica for drawing her into such a childish fight. Furious with Tom for not calling her. Furious with Nina for getting her into this situation. And furious with herself for falling madly in love with Ryan.

"Tell Denise Waters that Winston Egbert called," Winston shouted into the phone, growing increasingly frustrated by his inability to communicate with the Italian hotel operator.

"Momento."

Winston heard two loud female voices—sounding

226

an awful lot like Elizabeth and Jessica—coming from outside the beach house. Then he saw Ben come stomping back through the living room on his way to the kitchen. His face was an angry mask.

Winston lifted his eyebrows inquisitively, but Ben showed no interest at all in checking out the escalating hostilities outside.

There was a click, and another voice answered the line. This voice sounded slightly less perplexed. "*Allo.* You wish to leave message for Signorina Waters?"

"*Sì.*" Winston put the finger of his free hand into his ear to block the noise. "Tell her Winston Egbert called."

"Weldon Expert?"

"Close enough," he said. "*Grazie.*"

She'd barely popped the *P* on *prego* before he hung up and hurried to the door to investigate. "What in the . . ."

But before he took two steps, the door flew open with a bang. Wendy stood with her hands on her hips and her eyes blazing.

"You," she said in a voice thick with loathing.

Winston's heart sank. "Uh-oh."

"*Uh-oh* doesn't even begin to cover it," she said through clenched teeth.

"Now, Wendy," he placated, holding his hands protectively in front of him. "I don't know what happened, but I'm sure—"

"You liar!" she shouted, interrupting him.

"I meant well," he said lamely.

She moved toward him with her fists clenched. Winston backed cautiously around the edge of the sofa. "You meddling, lying crumb!"

Winston had never seen anybody look angry at him. "Please, Wendy. You're my best friend. . . ."

"Don't you *dare* call me friend."

The kitchen door swung open, and Ben came walking through with a large bag of chips cradled in his arm.

"Help!" Winston croaked.

But Ben seemed determined to ignore the tempests brewing inside and outside the house. He plopped down in the recliner with the paper, kicked it back, and stared determinedly at the front page of the newspaper.

"Do you have any idea how upset I am?" Wendy shouted.

"I'm getting a very good idea now." Winston scurried around the sofa, determined to stay out of reach.

Wendy reached down, grabbed a heavy sofa cushion, and flung it in his direction. He ducked and the sofa cushion hit the large ceramic lamp on the end table. It fell to the floor with a loud crash.

"I did not!" Winston heard Elizabeth yell as she walked in the front door.

"You did too!" Jessica shrieked.

When Winston turned his attention from the broken pottery on the floor toward the dueling

Wakefield twins, a second sofa cushion caught him on the side of the head and knocked him backward into Ben's arms.

"Look out!" Ben shouted.

The kitchen door swung open, and Paloma Perro came roaring out, barking ferociously and baring his fangs. He seemed determined to protect Wendy. His canine brain obviously pegged Winston as the threat, and he wasted no time in his approach, lunging for Winston's bare ankle.

Winston jumped to his feet, practically standing on Ben's chest.

"Get off me!" Ben shouted.

"Are you talking to me or the dog?" Winston shouted.

But Ben didn't answer because at that point the recliner tumbled over backward, taking them both with it.

"What the . . ." Nina heard the crash as soon as she opened the car door. She took off running toward the house, with Paul on her heels.

It sounded as if there were a tornado inside the house. Through the window she could see agitated figures in motion and hear shouts, screams, and the frantic barking of Paloma.

"Shut . . . up. Everybody shut up!" Nina heard Ben howl.

"I hate you!" Wendy's tearful falsetto soared over the others.

"Maybe there's been an accident," Nina panted, turning toward Paul.

"Sounds more like there's been a murder," Paul said.

Nina tore up the walk, yanked open the door, and watched, appalled, as Jessica, Elizabeth, Wendy, Winston, Ben, and Paloma Perro stood in the living room shouting, screaming, crying, barking, and waving their arms.

Sofa cushions were scattered in every corner. The recliner was overturned. The lamp beside the phone lay in shards on the floor.

The dog turned his face toward Nina and Paul and lifted his upper lip in a snarl.

Nina was so angry, she lifted her own lip and snarled back.

It must have been a pretty effective snarl because Paloma Perro's ears dropped, his tail lowered, and he let out a whine before ducking under the coffee table.

Emboldened by her success with the dog, Nina put her fingers to her lips and produced a loud, shrill whistle.

The group fell silent.

"What's going on here?" Nina demanded.

After a short pause everybody began talking at once. Jessica's tear-streaked face was red with anger.

Nina missed the first part but distinctly heard, "If I have to work with this back-stabbing, two-timing . . ."

Elizabeth's face showed no signs of tears, but she was obviously enraged herself and turned on Nina, saying something that went like, "Sick of you throwing your weight around. This has nothing to do with you, and I don't know why Jessica is even talking to you about—"

Ben waved his arms, determined to be heard. "I may have agreed to take Bryan's place, but I never agreed to spend the summer in a nuthouse, receiving emotional and verbal abuse—"

Behind them Wendy yelled at Winston, punctuating her sentence with blows with the sofa cushion. "Never . . . speak . . . to me . . . again!"

Winston's arms were folded over his head for protection, and he loudly protested his treatment.

Paul jumped into the fray and attempted to separate them, looking amused and alarmed at the same time.

Nina put her fingers to her lips and blew again. *"Quiet!"* she screamed, drawing out the word so long that she sounded like an air-raid siren.

Wendy paused in midpummel.

Jessica paused in midtirade.

Elizabeth paused in midsentence.

Ben blew out his breath in disgust.

And Winston raised his head, like a frightened turtle looking out of its shell.

Once she was satisfied that she had their full attention, Nina began. "I want everybody to relax and take ten deep breaths. Okay?"

The only sound now was the tentative *thump, thump* of Paloma Perro's tail on the floor.

"I mean it. Breathe!" Nina ordered.

The group reluctantly began to breathe while Nina counted. "One . . . two . . . three . . . four . . . five . . . six . . . seven . . . eight . . . nine . . . ten."

The oxygen had its desired effect and the hysteria level in the room dropped several degrees. Faces that had been angry began to look embarrassed.

"It's going to be a long summer," she said. "A long summer with heavy-duty responsibilities. Lifeguarding is a real job . . . and it takes teamwork. If we can't get along as housemates, we're never going to work effectively as teammates."

"You're right," Ben said. "So I'm going to resign."

"No, you're not," Nina argued.

Jessica folded her arms. "I'm resigning too."

"You're not," Nina announced in a voice that allowed no argument. "Nobody's going to resign. You people seem to be forgetting why you're here."

She walked to the hall storage closet, removed the broom and dustpan, and calmly began sweeping up the pieces of the broken lamp.

"Last summer a little girl drowned. Let me tell you something, the day you forget to take this job seriously, somebody pays. With their life. You guys have taken the training," Nina continued. "You've

232

been through the tryouts. Ryan spent a lot of time with you. So did I. You don't have any right to waste our time like that. You're the best on the beach, and you have an obligation and a duty to do the job now. You don't just get mad and walk away from it like some immature kid."

She set the dustpan full of glass on the table and leaned on the broom. "Some of us are old friends. Some of us are new friends. We're going to have our differences. There's no way around that. But those differences aren't very important compared to saving lives."

"You're right," Ben said.

"You'll stay?" Nina asked.

"I'll stay," Ben agreed.

"Jessica?"

"I'll stay too," she said quietly.

"Anybody else planing to leave?" Nina asked.

When nobody spoke up, she fixed each pair of eyes with a long and penetrating stare. "Okay, then. We're in it for the long haul. That means no matter what, through thick and thin, we're a team."

"I'm not even on the team. But I'll take the loyalty oath," Winston joked. He placed his hand on the broomstick over Nina's, like a baseball player swearing on a bat.

"Together." Ben grinned, grasping the pole above Winston's fist.

"Teammates," Elizabeth added.

"Friends," Wendy said. "Except with Winston Egbert, to whom I still am not speaking."

Paloma Perro let out a happy bark and then a startled yip when a loud, explosive noise shook the walls.

Jessica raced to the window. "What was that?"

Wendy shook her head. "I think it came from *inside*."

Ben cocked his head, listening. "Listen. It sounds like . . ." His eyes widened in alarm and he raced to the bathroom and threw open the door. "Oh, no!" he shouted.

A geyser of water spewed from the toilet toward the ceiling. A huge chunk of plaster had been knocked out of the ceiling when the lid to the toilet had blown off and sailed straight up.

"This is a disaster!" Ben exclaimed.

"Let's just hope it's not an omen." Winston groaned.

"Well, if it is," Wendy said, beginning to giggle, "it's a good one."

"How do you figure that?" Winston asked.

Wendy threw back her head and began to guffaw. "At least nobody was sitting on it."

Paloma thrust his head under her hand, and she petted his shaggy head. "Or drinking out of it," she added.

"I'll get the mop," Jessica said, running for the kitchen.

Ben ran behind her. "I'll get the tools."

Elizabeth began running up the steps. "We're going to need every towel we can find."

Nina watched the rising water level on the floor and smiled. The lease held them responsible for any and all damage to the property. They were racking up some bills tonight. But as far as Nina was concerned, it was money well spent. Because for the first time this summer, this mutinous group of squabbling housemates was working as a team.

Now that Jessica has caught Elizabeth kissing hunky head lifeguard Ryan Taylor, will she give up on him? Or will she fight even harder for the man of her dreams? Find out in Sweet Valley University #22, ELIZABETH'S SUMMER LOVE.

SIGN UP FOR THE SWEET VALLEY HIGH® FAN CLUB!

Hey, girls! Get all the gossip on Sweet Valley High's® most popular teenagers when you join our fantastic Fan Club! As a member, you'll get all of this really cool stuff:

- Membership Card with your own personal Fan Club ID number
- A Sweet Valley High® Secret Treasure Box
- Sweet Valley High® Stationery
- Official Fan Club Pencil (for secret note writing!)
- Three Bookmarks
- A "Members Only" Door Hanger
- Two Skeins of J. & P. Coats® Embroidery Floss with flower barrette instruction leaflet
- Two editions of *The Oracle* newsletter
- Plus exclusive Sweet Valley High® product offers, special savings, contests, and much more!

Be the first to find out what Jessica & Elizabeth Wakefield are up to by joining the Sweet Valley High® Fan Club for the one-year membership fee of only $6.25 each for U.S. residents, $8.25 for Canadian residents (U.S. currency). Includes shipping & handling.

Send a check or money order (do not send cash) made payable to "Sweet Valley High® Fan Club" along with this form to:

SWEET VALLEY HIGH® FAN CLUB, BOX 3919-B, SCHAUMBURG, IL 60168-3919

NAME_____
(Please print clearly)

ADDRESS_____

CITY_____ STATE_____ ZIP_____
(Required)

AGE_____ BIRTHDAY_____ /_____ /_____

Offer good while supplies last. Allow 6-8 weeks after check clearance for delivery. Addresses without ZIP codes cannot be honored. Offer good in USA & Canada only. Void where prohibited by law.
©1993 by Francine Pascal   LCI-1383-193